IN THEIR

In their Absence

HANNAH STEVENS

ROMAN BOOKS

ISBN 978-93-83868-59-9

Typeset in Adobe Garamond Pro and Bembo Std

First published in 2021

1 3 5 7 9 8 6 4 2

British Library Cataloguing in Publication Data
A catalogue record for this book is available from the British Library

Publisher: Suman Chakraborty

ROMAN Books
London | Kolkata
romanbooks.co.uk | romanbooks.co.in

STRETTO

A Fiction Series for ROMAN Books

Series Editor: Jonathan Taylor

'... a plurality of independent and unmerged voices and
consciousnesses.'

– Mikhail Bakhtin

Stretto is Italian for 'narrow' or 'close,' often used by musicians to
refer to climactic sections of fugues where the voices overlap more
closely, where the polyphonic texture is particularly intense. Stretto
is now also a ground-breaking series of novels, novellas and short
fictions, which takes on Mikhail Bakhtin's well-known conception
of 'polyphonic' literature, intensifying it, playing with it, developing
it in new contexts. Here are fictions which are multi-voiced, polyphonic, fugal in many different ways: fictions which are multi-
perspectival; fictions which stage clashing, sometimes dissonant
voices; fictions which hear from marginalised people; fictions which
interweave human voices and musical voices; fictions which engage
with voices from other places, other disciplines, other worlds. Above
all, here are stories which are themselves musical, lyrical, dynamically
contrapuntal.

This book is dedicated to

the missing,
the lonely
and the lost.

When you are gone,
 there'll be no answer to the questions —
the white clouds
 will go on and on forever.

Wang Wei (699-759)
Trans. Will Buckingham

Contents

Foreword

The UK National Police Chiefs' Council define a missing person as anyone whose whereabouts cannot be established, and where the circumstances are out of character or the context suggests they may be subject of a crime or at risk of harm to themselves or others.

In the UK 186,000 people are reported missing each year. For those who are left behind, often the worst thing is not the absence itself, but the absence of knowing. Why have these people gone missing? Where have they gone? Are they alive and will they return?

These stories are about missing people. They are an attempt to acknowledge the gaps, and to explore this absence and this unknowing.

Hannah Stevens,
2020

Swings

It's for the best, he says, and you say, I know. I know.

You're packing boxes: tomorrow you both leave. It's windy and you hear the chains of the swing set rattle in the breeze. It's easy to imagine your son is still here.

That night you go to bed with his teddy-bear and a t-shirt he wore the week he disappeared. These are the pieces of him left that you can hold.

In the morning, you take one last look at the garden. You notice the worn spots under the swings and how the grass is beginning to grow back.

Man Under

A woman followed him down the station steps to the side of the tracks. She liked his hat, a grey felt fedora and she wanted to touch it. He was drinking hot chocolate in a mug he'd brought from home. The drink smelled sweet and she wanted one but there wasn't enough time before the train came.

She saw his beige Mac billow out at both sides as he stepped down to the tracks. His hands were in his pockets and she wondered where his mug was. Then he just disappeared with the rush of the train. She could see the faces of the station crowd reflected in its black glass as the train slowed to a stop. Then she realised her hands were shaking.

'Man under! Man under!' Someone began to run along the platform towards the front of the train. Then other people started to move, to put their hands over their mouths, to catch the eyes of people next to them.

She wondered how it would've felt to step out knowing the impact was coming, knowing that you would be smeared along tracks like wet leaves. The impact of the train would've killed him quickly, maybe instantly. His organs would've burst like over-inflated balloons before the train got anywhere close to stopping.

It was then she turned and noticed his cup on the platform, placed neatly beneath a board that advertised a soon-to-be-best-selling book. She picked it up and held it in the circle of her hands. It was still warm.

People were shouting and their voices drifted up into the sky above them. The driver was off the train now, wrapped in a blanket that kept falling from his shoulders as he shivered. He couldn't keep his arms still and although his mouth moved there was no sound, as if every time he thought of a word it burst like a bubble on his tongue.

'It's your first one, isn't it?' said a man in station uniform. He stood next to the train driver and kept placing the blanket back on to his shoulders. He noticed a bird tattooed in shaky blue across the driver's hand: a swallow suspended in flight.

The woman who followed the man down to the platform and liked his felt fedora went home. She didn't wait for the next train which was diverted to another platform and she didn't go to work that day. Instead she walked slowly home with his cup in her right hand. She went back to bed and she slept for the rest of the day, dreaming of falling and of stairs that never ended.

The Soft Broken Parts

It didn't take them long to find his wallet and a couple of keys attached to a chain and suddenly the man under the train had a name: George.

George's wife woke up to the dial of her clock showing 8.32 in digital blue. George had kissed her goodbye an hour before and she thought he was going to work.

George's wife got out of bed and walked to the kitchen. She switched on the kettle. Out of the window the world looked colourful and she counted six shades of green in their small garden. Down the hallway and through the glass panels of the front door, she could see people walking to work.

She picked up her mobile phone from the kitchen sideboard. There was a message from George and in two lines of text the world was changed. He wrote about trains and goodbyes.

When the operator said, 'Emergency. Which service do you require?' George's wife didn't know what to say. Instead she talked about the felt fedora and then suicide and train tracks.

'He'll be wearing the hat. He always does. Send somebody quickly: maybe it isn't too late,' she said in a voice she'd never used before. The operator had taken a call about a man under the fast train to London just half an hour before. She already knew.

George's wife wanted everything back: his wallet and satchel, his hat and his shoes, and as many of his clothes as they could manage. But in the end the only things returned were his keys and a couple of coins thrown clear by the impact of the train. Everything else was too damaged, they said. She knew they would've had to peel and prise the soft, broken parts of him that were caught between wheels and tracks. She knew that everything would've been smashed and torn and that they probably wouldn't have recognised his hat as a hat when they'd picked it up, wouldn't have recognised George as George when they'd picked him up. They knew it was him, though: the dental records, the fingerprints they took said so.

Sometimes early in the morning she gets out of bed to touch his toothbrush, to see if it is wet. Sometimes she's sure that really he's just left for work, having washed his face and brushed his teeth. She opens and closes the cupboard above the sink. Pills he hadn't taken for weeks rattle in a bottle she'd found hidden at the back. Every day she picks it up and wonders how she didn't notice, wonders how she didn't know.

Bones

He noticed how she touched the barmaid's hand when she paid for her drink. Already he understood. It was in the way she breathed too: as if an ache stopped the muscles from expanding like they should. Tonight his loneliness made him brave. He touched her arm.

'I'm Henry,' he said, 'can I buy you a drink?'

Later, Bethan suggested a hotel.

'It would be sad to say goodbye so early,' she said. 'Aren't we having a good time?'

This had never happened to him before. He wasn't that kind of man. Except tonight there was no reason to say no, and so he nodded his head, followed her.

'Do you have a room high up?' she asked the reception staff as they booked in, 'one where we can see the whole of the sky?'

The boy behind the counter paused, checked his screen. 'No problem,' he said, and he gave them the key.

The hotel room is blue. It reminds Henry of hospital visits. Maybe this isn't a good idea but it feels too late to say no. He can hear something buzzing now the door is closed and he looks over to the window. A wasp crawls across the glass. Bethan opens the sash and they watch it fly away.

Her skin is cold at first but soon there is heat beneath his fingertips. She's taken off her clothes and he thinks that she's lovely, although a little thin. He can feel her ribs and he shakes now that he holds her. He can't decide whether he should hold her more tightly or touch her more lightly. The bed sinks beneath them and the springs press into his back.

Henry runs his fingertips along her spine and then holds her hips. They are sharp in his hands and he'd forgotten how this feels.

Afterwards, when they smoke together she opens the window wider, pushes the sash upwards, as high as it will go. There should probably be a safety catch but there's nothing, and he thinks it opens too far.

They've been drinking for hours now, snorting the cocaine from the small bag she pulled from her bra. She pours them the last of the wine and Henry realises it's light outside. He hears cars, and birds beginning to sing. She's talking quickly, and he can't decide exactly why but he thinks that she looks different to yesterday.

She swallows the last of her drink and he looks at the empty bottles across the room. It takes him a minute to realise what she's saying, even though she's talking slowly and the words are simple and neat in her mouth. She tells him about the time she laid down one night in the freezing cold. She'd taken off her clothes and there'd been a frost. It was in a park not far from where she used to live, a few months after her baby died.

'Can you believe I woke up the next day?' she asks. 'It was as if nothing had happened.'

Henry doesn't answer because he doesn't know what to say. There are two rolled up notes beside her. The white powder has gone now and he's glad. She tells him about her husband who destroyed her with other women and then she sits on the sill and points to her face.

'He used to tell me how beautiful this was,' she says. 'Not any more.' He wants to touch her again but she seems so far away. This is the story of his life: if only he was brave enough to stand up and move towards her. He notices a rash on her throat: a flush of red across the pale skin. The sky is silver and flat and the smoke she blows from her mouth rushes through the open window.

'My baby was called Gabriel,' she says. 'But now he's dead.' She throws the cigarette from the window and lights another with a match made of black wood. She'd picked the matches up from the bar as they left. He'd noticed her nails and the white half-moons in them as she closed her palm around the box. He imagines that her hands feel cold now because it is cold outside. He thinks of her wet mouth less than an hour before; remembers how it was warm.

She's quiet then, moves her hand to just below her nose, holds it there. When she takes it away, Henry sees there's blood on her face.

'This runs in the family,' she says, 'my daughter gets nosebleeds too.' And then she laughs, but he doesn't get the joke. He understands that things are beginning to swerve out of control and he doesn't know what he should do.

He hesitates, hands her a tissue. He watches the clock on the wall as he waits for the bleeding to stop. He tells her how he's sorry for everything; sorry for it all, and if only things could be different.

He hears the traffic outside but the room is silent.

Bethan leans out of the sash window, looks at the sky, looks down.

'Do you know that birds have hollow bones so they can fly?' she says. Henry shakes his head. He's never thought of this before.

Bethan leans out further and further again. There's a blur of flesh and a rush of air. Henry stands and reaches out for her, but she has already gone and there is nothing for him to hold.

Gabriel

The light was so bright that the birds thought it was sunrise and began to sing. There was ash in the air and a small girl called Kristie stood on the grass and watched as the house burned.

Neighbours ran from their front doors and watched. A man held the small girl's mother, grasped her arms as she tried to twist away and run towards the house. After a few minutes she began to scream and her legs bent beneath her as she fell to the floor. The man thought of just-born baby cows stumbling on shaking legs and for a second he looked away as she lay on the grass. The flames were high above the house now and the sky was orange. The birds were right, it looked like sunrise.

'Gabriel!' the girl's mother screamed. But they all knew Gabriel wasn't coming out. The fire engine arrived seven minutes after the call, and firefighters in dark overalls pushed people away from the house.

'Get back!' they shouted and held their arms high above their heads. The crowd could feel the heat from the fire on their faces and they stepped back to the pavement across the street. Red sparks fluttered through the air. They caught in Kristie's hair.

'Hold on,' said a man who lived across the road. He looked at Kristie and she stayed where she was. The sleeve of his shirt felt soft as he pulled it across her mouth; she hadn't noticed that her nose was bleeding until then. The man held his cuff under her nose and they waited for the blood to stop coming.

Soon there were paramedics. People in green carried Kristie's mother to the back of an ambulance and said her name over and over again.

'Bethan, can you hear me? Bethan?'

Kristie thought the name sounded strange repeated again and again; it lost more of its meaning each time the strangers said it out loud.

There was almost nothing left by the time it was light. Just black bricks and cinders that stayed hot for days. They found Gabriel in the early hours: the fire crew said he'd crawled beneath his bed and hidden there. They put the burned body into a tiny box and carried him to a dark car. The box was grey like ash and somehow that hadn't seemed right at all. It was raining by then and the street was silver and wet. The neighbours had waited all night for the flames to die and they shivered. They began to wonder if anybody had thought to call Alex. He was Gabriel's father, after all, and someone should tell him the news; someone should tell him to come home.

Five weeks later they buried Gabriel in a service where there was no God. They played two sad songs and talked of injustice and how time heals all things. He had a coffin lined with velvet and a stone that said his name in gold leaf. The day smelt of damp soil and lilies and Bethan's mouth was cracked and white.

Alex didn't know Gabriel was dead until he got home. It was late evening and he found his house empty and dark: a shell of black gaps and missing windows. Nobody had called him because nobody knew where he was. He could still smell the smoke as he walked towards the house and for a few minutes thought the taxi had dropped him on the wrong street.

His trips away stopped after that, and Kristie noticed how her father didn't smell of women's perfume any more. Now there was silence where before there had always been fighting and tears.

'Does she fuck you better than I do?' Bethan always asked when he got home after a few days away. Alex always noticed how her shoulders were hard and tense when she shouted. 'You fuck strangers in expensive hotels while I'm up all night wondering who you're with and if she looks like me. What kind of welcome home do you expect?'

'What do you want me to say, Bethan? They never last. It's only a game, just something fun.' He was always calm when he spoke, as if he was right. She didn't need to worry. He wasn't the type of man to run out on his family because he'd chosen his wife on a whim and sometimes regretted it. He always came home in the end and didn't that mean he was a good man really? If there was a thing called love, then this was the closest thing to it.

A year after the fire Bethan left. She didn't pack a bag, didn't leave a note. A neighbour from across the road had watched as Bethan left the house and walked down the street. It was early in the morning and the birds had just begun to sing. When she turned the corner the neighbour realised Bethan wasn't wearing any shoes. It was too late to call her by then: she was too far away.

Every year Kristie visits Gabriel's grave and wonders if she should miss someone she never really knew. She places flowers on top of soil that's full of weeds and they reflect in the marble: a halo of colour across the black headstone. Kristie thinks of the flames as they burned across the night sky and made the birds sing: sometimes it's as though she's been staring at the burning house all her life.

The Moon was Low and Close

Her bed was warm and through the crack in the curtains she could see stars stamped across the hard, black sky. She turned over and looked at the clock. The digital display was green and it glowed midnight. Her mobile phone was ringing and she picked it up.

'Lydia, it's Felix,' the voice said. 'The car has come off the road into a ditch and I can't get it out. I'm not too far from home but not walking distance. Can you come and pick me up?'

'Where are you?' she asked. 'Were you driving too fast?'

'No,' he said, 'I don't know what happened exactly but I think the tyre blew out. The car turned over on its side and I had to climb out. But don't worry. I'm fine - just cold and a bit shaken.'

'Okay, I'll get dressed and jump in the car now. Whereabouts are you?'

'Well it's dark but I think I'm on Gartree Road. All I can see is fields but I'm sure I passed a sign not long ago. I'll stay by the car. You can just about see it from the road as you're driving. But I'll move further out when I hear you coming.'

'I'm getting up now,' she said. 'I won't be long.'

Lydia took off her pyjamas, pulled on jeans from the bedroom floor. She shivered as the cold material settled around her legs. Her eyes were beginning to adjust to the dark and she saw her breath form white clouds in front of her face. She pulled a jumper over her head and picked up the coat hanging on the bedroom door. Then she pushed her phone deep into a pocket and ran down the stairs.

Outside the moon was low and close and beneath its white light the street sparkled. Lydia hesitated for a second before she turned the key in the ignition: everywhere was so quiet and still. She scraped the ice from the windscreen until her fingers ached and then she climbed inside the car. She turned the heater to full and she sat and waited for the glass to clear.

There was no traffic and it didn't take long to leave the bright city streets, to pass into the darker, twisting country roads and to find the road where Felix said he was. Trees crowded inward, formed a canopy above her and in some places they blocked the light of the moon. She was close to the pub they'd often visited together when her phone began to ring. She took it from her pocket and the screen glowed: *Felix*.

'Hello,' she said, 'I've just passed the pub. It took a while to get off the drive because I had to de-ice the car. The roads are quiet, though, so I won't be long.'

'I've started to walk,' he said, 'I was too cold standing still and I don't like the noises from the trees.'

'What noises?' she asked.

He laughed.

'I don't know. It's dark and probably just the wind. I'm scaring myself over nothing. I think my nerves are frayed from spinning off the road. Anyway I'm walking now. It should be in the direction you're coming from if I've worked out where I am properly.' She could hear in his voice that he was walking fast: he was slightly out of breath.

'Okay,' she said, 'see you soon.' She ended the call and put the phone back into her pocket. The heater was blowing hot now and she turned it down. The zip of her coat dug into her throat and she coughed. There was a gap in the trees and the moon shone. Its light haloed across the sky and she thought of work the next day and how she would be tired.

How long had she been driving now? She looked at the clock: fifteen minutes had passed. This was the stretch of road where Felix said he would be, but there'd been no sign of him yet. Maybe she'd been driving too fast. Maybe she'd passed him already? Despite the heat in the car, she shivered.

'Hello, Felix, I'm on the road where you said. I've been driving for fifteen minutes now. I thought I would have found you.'

'Just keep going, you can't be far. I'm still walking.' He sounded impatient this time. And was there panic in his voice? She couldn't decide.

'Are you walking in the right direction?'

'Yes,' he said, 'I was just further back than I thought. These country roads all look the same. Have you noticed how low the moon is? It's giving me a shadow. I never realised you could cast a shadow in the dark.'

'Felix,' she said, although she didn't quite know why.

'I'll keep walking,' he said, 'you won't miss me. Don't worry.'

Lydia locked the car doors.

A few minutes passed and then, what was that? Lydia saw the tyre tracks on the road. They veered towards trees across grass that was slashed with mud.

The car. No Felix. It took her a few seconds to stop.

She pulled over. The wind was icy when she stepped outside and it took her breath. She moved towards the car although she wasn't sure what she was looking for. Of course he wasn't there and for a second she didn't move.

The car radio was smashed, the display off and yet twisted high-pitched notes crowded the air. The wind picked up the noise, scattered it amongst the trees. Lydia turned the volume button but the sound stayed the same. She wondered how long a car battery took to die.

Back at the roadside Lydia held her phone in a shaking hand, pressed it to the side of her head. She listened to the ringing and she waited but this time Felix did not answer.

Drought

I've been missing for months: here, nobody knows who I am.

We're in the middle of a drought: everything is drying up and burning down.

At the party I catch a man's green eyes and eat from his paper plate. He has black hair and doesn't remind me of home. I follow him outside and we kiss on the step.

Later, the last bits of light fade away and, in the tangle of sheets, I try to show him what it means to touch me. I love his weight on my bones, his breath on my neck. I wonder how long he will stay for.

In the morning he asks for water. He takes the glass and drinks to the bottom.

I follow him to the door and he doesn't look back as he leaves.

The Call of the Circus

She didn't know they were coming but she knew when they'd arrived. It was April and the weather was too good for the time of year.

She heard the noise on the breeze: the faint, twisted sound of faraway music from a tent. She was outside and sat on steps framed by wisteria. Purple flowers hung from the thin tangled limbs of the plant and the heavy bunches reminded her of grape vines. Her feet were pale and bare and the tops of them burned.

Every few minutes there was a lyric caught between the music in the air. Adel put on her shoes and began to walk towards the music. As a child she'd felt compelled to follow ice-cream vans and her mother had lost her more than once. It had never been the sweet things that drew her. They'd always hurt her teeth: it was the colour and noise that she'd had to chase.

The circus tent stood in the fields across the main road. It was tall and she could see the red top and stripes high above street signs and hedges. The sky above it was dark blue but faded to paler shades as it got closer to the earth. It hadn't rained for weeks and the dust in the air turned orange in the falling sun.

'We're eating outside tonight,' Adel said, 'you just need to bring the wine and glasses.' She handed Noah a cold, cloudy bottle from the fridge and watched as the condensation ran down its neck. It was Sunday and he'd been working overtime again. Outside, she'd already lit the barbeque and the coals were silver and hot. She'd laid coloured bowls of salad and rice on the table and chopped radishes in the shape of jagged flower heads.

'Oh,' he said, 'but what about the insects: I'll be bitten all over.' He looked at her but she was already in the arch of the door.

'There's something in the cupboard for that,' she said without turning her head. 'I'll see you outside.'

It was past ten now and though the garden was dark the sky still had patches of blue. It was as if day was waiting for something and wouldn't leave.

'Look at that,' Adel said and pointed upwards.

'Beautiful,' he said and looked at her in that way he always did when he wanted something. She picked up the folded blanket beside her and pulled it across her legs.

She remembered the time she'd thought she was pregnant. It wasn't that long ago and she remembered the sick feeling and how she couldn't bear to do a test. Instead she'd looked up abortion clinics and how they did it. When Noah asked what made her restless at night she'd said it was work. Or maybe she was eating too late. It was probably just one of those things, you know how it is. In the end there'd been nothing to worry about. Either she'd miscounted the dates or nature had solved the problem for her.

'Shall we go inside?' he said. 'I think I've been bitten. Plus we've both got early starts tomorrow and you look tired.'

She thought of the drive to work in the morning and reading the same street names as she passed them. She thought of the traffic crawling at its painful pace during rush hour and parents at school gates with purple shadows beneath their eyes.

'You go,' she said, 'I'm staying out a little bit longer.'

'What about the cleaning up?' he asked.

'It can wait,' she said. 'Let's be reckless.' She picked up her glass then and swallowed the last of the wine.

'Okay, just this once,' he laughed and then he kissed her nose which felt cold now.

She waited until she heard the click of the door as it closed. Then she stood up and crossed the garden. The grass was cool and she could feel the material of her canvas shoes dampen as she walked. She stopped at the top of the driveway. A few seconds passed. There was still the sound of music but it was fainter now: maybe the circus had finished for the night. She hesitated for a moment and then stepped onto the pavement.

There were caravans lined up in neat rows behind the circus tent. In some she could see lights glowing from behind drawn curtains while others were in darkness. She wondered who was inside and if any of them were sleeping yet. There was noise coming from the circus tent and the music was louder there. She pushed aside the material that had been untied from its guy ropes and now hung across the entrance.

String lights were suspended from the ceiling and curled around supporting poles and ropes. They were shaped like lanterns and glowed red, yellow, green and blue. There were clowns in the centre of the tent and she watched as they stacked chairs and put props into boxes. Adel noticed a pile of empty beer bottles.

'Are you okay?' a clown in braces with bare feet asked.

'Yes', she said, 'I was just having a look.'

'Well the show's over now, you missed it,' said the clown, 'but you can join us for a drink if you want.' The clown gestures towards seats close to where Adel stood. She took a few steps and sat down. The clown offered her a bottle of beer and she leant forward to take it.

It was hot in the tent: a humid heat and Adel tasted salt on her lips. The clowns were still wearing their makeup and she wondered if she would recognise any of them once they'd taken it off. The clown next to Adel had smudged some of the white paint across her face and flashes of peach showed across her forehead.

Someone turned up the music.

'Let's dance,' said the clown with the smudged makeup. She held out her hand as if inviting Adel to a formal waltz. Adel laughed and stood up. The clown's hand was cool in spite of the heat and Adel was surprised.

'When are you leaving?' Adel said.

'Tomorrow,' said the clown and raised an eyebrow. 'In the morning when most people will still be asleep.' Adel could feel her phone as it buzzed in her pocket but she doesn't answer. The clown's shirt was undone now and there was a vest Adel could see through beneath. A giant blue bow was still tied across her throat and Adel touched it. It was soft between her fingertips.

'That soon?' Adel asked.

'Yes,' said the clown and she pulled Adel closer. 'Come with us.'

The Best Way to Kill a Butterfly

For reasons nobody seemed sure of, butterflies filled the skies like flocks of birds that summer. Young children stood on streets with arms extended, their sleeves covered with fluttering wings. National newspapers ran the story on their front pages and footage was played over and over on television screens. Temperatures were the hottest on record but Tess wore black and let her skin burn. It was the summer Madeline would've been born.

The street where Tess lived was wide and leafy and in the front garden there was a buddleia bush she didn't cut back any more. In the cooler spring she'd noticed how the dark leaves had been eaten away to heart shaped skeletons. The chrysalises of hundreds of caterpillars had hung from the green spines of the leaves. It was a surprise to see the branches foam with purple flowers when summer came. Across the road there was a park and people with pushchairs and cameras came to visit the expanse of well-tended flowerbeds. They'd disappear a few hours later with blistered skin and photographs of butterflies and bright blossoms on bare, leafless stalks.

Every day that summer, Tess got home to find butterflies fluttering against the opaque panes of the bathroom window. She wondered how they could be so blind and why, after so many attempts at the same piece of glass, they didn't look for another way out. The first time it happened she was home late. Work was busy and she didn't rush to get back to an empty house. Walking into the bathroom she saw the butterfly's silhouette, dark against the sun that still shone through the glass. There were lilac eyes on its wings. The fur on its body shivered in a slight breeze. She fetched a mug from the kitchen cupboard and picked up an envelope from the sideboard.

Then she stepped onto the edge of the bath and leant forward to place the mug over its body. The plastic ledge was slippery and her bare feet began to slide. She fell forward and the mug hit the window. As her temple hit the tap she heard the ceramic smash on the floor. The butterfly landed silently on the tiles.

Michael had left days ago and so nobody came to see what the noise was or if she was okay.

It was a few minutes before Tess sat up. The butterfly's antennae still twitched: its torn-away wing lay on the windowsill. Tess picked up a flat shard of the broken mug and pressed it quickly over its body. There was a noise like the crumpling of paper.

After that, Tess kept the windows closed. She checked them twice and turned the latch to *locked* whenever she left the house. But every day she came home to the faint noise of wings fluttering against glass. She would catch them in her hands now and their wings felt like feathers in her palms. She would take them outside and throw them towards the sky, like she had hands full of confetti.

Soon there were stories about a new craze. It was on the front page of every newspaper: people talked about it wherever you went. The butterflies could be pressed between glass and mounted in frames you could hang in your hallways. They could be trapped in pendants made with silver and varnish and threaded onto chains you wore around your neck. Small ones could be fashioned into rings for your fingers. Why wouldn't you want your own piece of this pretty phenomenon? There were enough of them to go around, after all. The how-to guides said the killing method was simple. You did it like this:

> *The best way to kill a butterfly is to pinch its thorax between your thumb and forefinger. The thorax is the middle segment of the butterfly's body and is the fattest part of the insect. You must learn the correct pressure and this technique takes practice. It will stun the specimen and prevent it from*

damaging itself. The specimen can then be slipped into an envelope or a tight-fitting box with insecticide and kept indefinitely until mounted or made into jewellery.

For those who want to add caterpillars to their collection it is advisable to drown them in a preservative fluid or to boil them like shrimp.

At dinner parties it became customary to have butterfly centrepieces. The insects would be pinned to cork and encased in beautiful frames. After eating, guests were given nets and jars and there were competitions over who could catch the one considered the prettiest. Those who took part chose between Red Admirals, purple-eyed Peacocks and Orange Monarchs with wings like stained glass windows. Cabbage Whites were mostly left alone or given to children as tiny trophies for good behaviour. Winners got to keep their butterfly and were issued with pins and boards to make their own souvenir when they got home. Runners-up left their dead butterflies on sideboards or patio slabs to be swept and tidied away the next day.

Tess was going to be late for dinner. She'd got away from work on time but the heat was heavy and thick and it made her move slowly. Upstairs she'd opened the sash window and sat on her bed. The blankets were warm from the sunshine and she took off her clothes. Outside there was the noise from the road. She could hear the wheels of pushchairs and people talking and she could see the features of their faces. There were curtains at the window but she didn't close them. She knew that if they looked up towards her window they would see her and she wondered what they would think if they did. She would shower soon and get ready to go out. But first she would lie down for a few minutes and maybe she would fall asleep. It didn't matter that she would arrive late because she knew that everyone would say, *it's okay, Tess, we understand.* The sun shone through the window and fell across her shoulders. She closed her eyes and in a few minutes her skin began to burn.

36

When she woke, her shoulders were sore. She turned her head and saw the red mark across her skin. She stood and stretched. Her scalp felt tight and she could feel the heat from the sun beneath her hair: the back of her head was burnt too. Outside she saw Drew from next door. He was back from work and he locked his car. Tess stepped towards the window and he turned towards the house. She watched him look up but she didn't move. She knew that he could see her.

'You're so late,' said Tess's friend when she opened the front door, 'I didn't think you were coming.'

'I fell asleep when I got home from work,' said Tess, 'and look: I got burnt from lying in the sun.' Tess turned away then to show her the red patches across her shoulder blades. As she turned, her friend placed her palm onto the green wood of the door. Tess heard it click into place as it closed and she saw a ring on her hand.

'What do you think?' she said. The black and blue butterfly wing was cased in clear resin and mounted on silver. 'I found it in the garden – on the buddleia bush. I pinned the butterfly to the board and took off the wing myself,' she said.

There was bottle of white wine in Tess's hand and the glass felt cold and slippery in her fingers. She wondered if the butterflies bled when people put pins in them and, even if they did, if anyone noticed. 'I took the wing to the jeweller on the same day because I already knew what I wanted. She said it was a really neat cut when I got there. Nothing torn or frayed and it was perfectly intact. Isn't it beautiful?'

'It's not really my taste,' said Tess. Her friend was silent and for a second she looked at her as if she didn't understand. The bottle began to slip from Tess's hand but she didn't tighten her grip. She felt it slide from her grasp and the glass smashed when it hit the coloured tiles of the floor. She bent down and put a piece in her palm.

'Fuck,' said Tess's friend, 'don't move. Your sandals are so thin you'll get something stuck in your foot. Wait here while I get a brush. Don't worry, we all know it's been a difficult time for you.'

Tess could hear voices from the back rooms.

'When are we catching these butterflies?' someone said, 'And does the winner get a bottle of wine too?' There was the sound of laughing. Tess opened the front door and stepped quietly onto the street.

After it happened it was as if Michael had got up and left. It was as if they both had except they were still there. When they ate it was like they weren't really eating at all, because food tasted of nothing and it was difficult to swallow. And when they fucked, it was like they weren't really fucking at all. They would twist and kneel in their usual positions and sometimes they made a noise so they could pretend they were having fun. But what they were really thinking about was how long it would be before they could go to sleep.

Tess hadn't seen Michael cry since it happened. Or get angry. She wondered if he blamed her and she hoped that he did because she wanted to be blamed.

The bedroom window was open and in the heat and the darkness there was the smell of blossom. They were in bed and fucking and in the dark she couldn't make out his face. She looked down and traced the silhouette of his head against the pillows. He was quiet aside from his breathing which was only a little faster than when he was beginning to fall asleep. *He's barely here*, she'd thought and then she'd wanted to hurt him. She'd moved quickly, bending her knees, kneeling on his chest and pressing down with all her weight. He'd said something she couldn't make out and then she'd bitten his lip hard between her teeth. He inhaled sharply and she pushed down harder so the air rushed from his mouth. For a few seconds they didn't move.

There was no air in his lungs and her weight pressed him to the bed. He felt his heart begin to beat faster. Blood rushed in his ears and his lip throbbed. He felt her breath on his face and he began to panic then and pushed her.

There was a thud when she fell to the floor, but otherwise she didn't make a sound. At the window he saw moths fluttering at the glass of the raised sash. There was a streetlight outside and they tried to get to it. Michael felt sick and the heat of the room made it hard for him to catch his breath. Tess stood and moved to the arch of the door. He noticed that she walked slowly and held her arm but he didn't ask where it hurt or if she was okay.

In the bathroom she switched on the light. She turned towards the mirror and saw that there was a bruise coming. She'd landed on her shoulder and it felt full of knots and aches. She imagined that there would be patches of purple and blue down to her elbow soon and she thought that it felt good to feel hurt in some other way. She waited in the doorway for him to say something: for him to call her a fucking bitch and ask what she thought she was doing, but he didn't. He stayed silent on the bed and so she walked away. She slept on the settee for the rest of the night. The leather cushions felt cool beneath her and when she woke up she felt cold and she shivered.

Michael heard her close the bathroom door and walk downstairs. He switched on the light and looked for his bag. He chose a pair of shoes from the bottom of the wardrobe, then trousers, shorts, some shirts, a hat. He laughed: it was like packing for a holiday, except he wasn't. Tomorrow he'd catch the train and get off at the coast. It didn't matter which one so he'd choose the one with the cheapest fare. When he left she'd be glad, because the silences won't be heavy and tense and at night she can go to sleep with the light on.

At the coast Michael had expected fewer butterflies. But there were fields and flowers and trees close to the sea and so the butterflies filled the sky like at home. He saw gulls at the beach swoop and catch them in their beaks. The sun burned in the sky and he was glad he was wearing his hat. Children were building sandcastles and eating sandwiches. People were paddling and taking photographs. He stepped onto the sand and it felt hot beneath his bare feet. As he neared the sea he noticed that tangled in the seaweed and the shale were the faded, broken wings of butterflies. He bent down and picked one up. It turned to powder in his fingertips and left sharp grains of sand in his hands.

The water was cold in spite of the sun and his feet ached as he stepped under the waves. As he walked, he turned to see the beach behind him. The wind blew in the wrong direction for him to hear but he saw a child crying. The child's mother tried to swat away butterflies that crowded around the sticky, white ice cream the child had in his hands. The butterflies launched and darted towards the cone and he had never seen them move like that before. He wondered what they usually ate and if it was the sugar or the coolness that they liked in the scorching heat. The mother waved her hands and he thought of dancing and of being drunk. The child dropped the ice cream and Michael watched as the mother stamped on the mush of white and sand and butterflies. He turned away and traced the line on the horizon where the sea met the sky.

Michael's B&B was cheap: the curtains faded, the carpet garish and worn. It was still light when he checked in. Dust motes caught in the slices of sun that fell through the grimy windows. There was no view of the sea from here: the receptionist didn't think he looked like the kind of man who would care.

Michael was on his knees and fucking a woman he doesn't love from behind. There was a circus in town and that's where they'd met. Michael thought of the flashing lights, the drum rolls and the cold beer he drank straight from the can. He thought of the rose he caught, thrown in to the crowd during one of the shows, and how he offered it to her because she was sat next to him and he didn't know what else to do with it.

'You really shouldn't have,' she said and then she laughed.

'What's your name?' he asked.

'Adel,' she said.

'Are you on holiday here?' he asked.

'Kind of,' she said, 'but mostly I'm just sleeping with one of the clowns.'

When they'd finished fucking she stood up, smiled.

'I ran away from home and my husband to be with a circus clown,' she said, and then she laughed. Michael lies down on the bed and pulls the sheet over his chest. He doesn't know this woman and he hasn't done this for a long time. He doesn't know if he should hold her and he isn't sure that he wants to. She begins to get dressed.

'The clown is a woman, you know. But sometimes…,' she pauses, 'I wonder that I might miss this.' She gestures towards him and then pulls on her t-shirt. 'But I've decided that I don't, in case you wondered. It's just, I needed to feel sure. And now I know, so thank you.' He doesn't know what he should say to this but it's okay because now she's kissing him. Her tongue is in his mouth and it tastes sweet and then she says goodbye and closes the door behind her.

By mid-September torn wings and mashed bodies of butterflies blew through the streets. The newly dead squelched and slipped underfoot while older ones rustled and crunched like dead leaves. Tess was in the garden hanging out sheets that smelt of lime. There were voices and she looked across the low fence. It was Tom and his dad, Drew. She wondered how old Tom was and guessed that it was somewhere around five. She watched as Tom's father took a butterfly from the net in his hand and slowly squeezed its middle. There was a pop as its abdomen burst and she watched as its black body turned to a sticky mess between his fingers. Tom squealed and it reminded Tess of the slaughterhouse noises her father had told her about.

'Don't worry, son, we'll soon catch another one,' Tom's father said as he wiped the black smudge onto his jeans. Tess noticed Drew's hands and how they were tanned. She wondered how his fingers would feel in her mouth and then she stepped closer to the fence.

She watched as the boy walked back inside. His face was pink and hot and she knew that he was about to cry.

'Hello,' she said, 'how's the butterfly catching going?'

Drew turned around.

'Hello,' he said, 'not that great actually. Well, the catching is okay – they're slow and stupid because of the heat. And obviously there are so many of them that they'd be difficult to miss. It's just, I keep squashing them.' He checked his thumb and pulled a face at the dark stain on his fingers. 'We've never spoken before, have we?' he said and she knew this wasn't really a question.

41

'No,' she said, 'though I've seen you from my window and heard Tom calling your name.' She watched him blush. 'It's been a strange time. I'm sorry I haven't introduced myself. Welcome to the street.' She laughed then and made a gesture with her arm. He smiled and dropped the net he'd been holding to the floor.

'Thanks,' he said, 'and yes, these are strange times.' He pointed to the butterflies that had landed on his chest. Tess counted six of them and then nodded, although that wasn't what she meant.

There were birds on the grass: a female chaffinch and her orange mate. They were fat because of the good summer and Tess saw them crumpling butterflies in their beaks as they ate them.

'I'm here alone at the moment,' she said. 'Michael has left and I don't know if he's coming back.'

'Oh,' said Drew, 'I'm sorry,' and he noticed that there was a ring with a diamond on her left hand.

'Are you free later?' she said. He looked at her then, right in her eyes, and he understood that she was offering him something.

'I can come over for eight,' he said, and he didn't even pause before he said this.

'I'll leave the door unlocked,' she said and then she turned and finished hanging the sheets on the line.

It's cooler in the house and Drew is glad. He watches her from the window in the kitchen. It doesn't take her long to string the washing from the cord that stretches across the garden. She's hanging bed sheets and pillow cases and they are all black. He has never laid on black sheets before and he wonders if tonight he will. Abby is in the living room and he can hear that the television is on. Tom has stopped crying over the crushed butterfly. Drew wonders what he will tell them when he leaves to go next door, when he leaves to do something he will never want them to know about.

It is still light when Tess hears the door being pushed open from the outside. She swallows the last of the wine in her glass and puts it onto the coffee table.

'Hello,' he says. His voice is quiet and it shakes at the edges. She stands and walks across the carpet with bare feet. She knows he won't be able to hear her yet because she is too far away. He hasn't moved since he closed the door and she knows that the hallway will seem dim now he is inside. She wonders what her house smells like to him and if he's looked up the stairs towards her bedroom. She wants to get to him before he speaks again: she thinks it will be better if they don't talk. She stands in the doorway and he sees her. She puts her finger across her closed lips and Drew understands what this means. His hands shake as he places them on to her hips and he hopes she doesn't notice.

Later when Drew goes home there's a scratch that traces from his shoulder blade down to his thigh. He knows that it's there but he doesn't see it until the next day when he's in the bathroom with the door locked. He wonders how long it will take to fade.

It was dark when he got home and the house was quiet and still. Abby was asleep in their bed and she felt warm when he slid in beside her. Usually he slept naked when it was hot, but tonight he wore his t-shirt and felt glad that Tess didn't wear perfume.

That morning Michael called Tess and asked if he could come home. His voice was quiet and broken on the phone and he was sorry. He'd called her from a pay phone because he'd lost his mobile, and can you believe they even still exist he'd asked.

'It's lucky that they do,' she said.

'And what about all the butterflies?' he said, 'There's still so many of them, even now.'

'I know,' said Tess. 'And isn't it sad what people are doing to them?'

She hadn't blamed him for leaving. It'd been difficult to find the words afterwards. What did people expect? Michael had woken to screams in the night as Tess almost bled to death on their sheets. A few minutes later there had been something small like a doll that, for a minute or two, had felt warm when Michael had held her. They'd called her Madeline and she was buried in a coffin Michael had carried in his hands. Nothing was going to be okay after that.

Madeline's room was mostly empty now. The pile of the carpet was deep and warm under Tess's feet and there was a teddy bear that wore a silk ribbon. As she'd stepped through the door, Tess had heard the noise of wings beating against glass. She'd stepped forward as the butterfly landed and she watched as it tapped quickly across the panes. Michael was coming home today. He'd asked her if he could and she'd said yes, that she wanted him here. The summer was beginning to fade away, and wasn't autumn their favourite time? Tess unlocked the heavy brass catch of the frame and pushed open the window. The breeze was cooler than it had been for months and she felt the hairs rise on her arms. She stood then, with her palm on the cold wall and she watched as the pale Cabbage White fluttered out into the wide, silver sky.

Shadows

He realises that over an hour has passed. It's gone midnight, almost one o'clock. Noah opens the back door and steps outside. Today has been too hot and he has a headache. It's cooler now and he's glad. The hair on his bare arms rises, he shivers.

'Adel,' he calls through the shadows. 'Adel, are you coming in?' Outside the security light doesn't switch on: he's been meaning to mend it. It takes a few seconds for his eyes to adjust to the dark and he follows the flagstone path through the centre of the grass. The air is damp now and his shoes slide on the stones as he walks. He sees the darker shadows of their empty chairs against the hedge. The blanket she had across her lap is on the floor: he picks it up and it feels cold.

'Adel?' There's no answer. He feels something heavy gathering around him and for a second he loses his breath.

'Adel?' he's louder this time but his voice fades quickly and he hears tree branches crack above his head. His stomach tightens. He walks quickly now, scanning the garden, looking behind the trees near the sun porch because maybe she's hiding and this is a joke. She'll appear soon: they'll go inside and go to bed together where it's warm and they won't wear any clothes.

'Adel, are you there? This isn't funny now.' He's jogging, scanning the darkness for shadows that move, or shadows that don't move but shouldn't be there. He sees nothing, runs across the gravel of the driveway towards the gate. The street is empty: there's the sound of passing traffic from the main road a short walk away and he hears the fading music from the circus in the field behind.

There's sweat on his top lip in spite of the cold and Noah wipes it with the back of his hand.

Maybe she came inside and he didn't see her. Maybe he'd fallen asleep and missed the noise of her as she closed the door. He climbs the stairs quickly already knowing she's not there. The bed is empty: there's no-one.

He picks up his phone and calls her mobile. It feels hot against his ear and there's no answer.

His hands sweat and for the first time in his life he presses 999.

He waits at the gate for them to come. There's no house number and now it's dark they might miss the turn from the road. He doesn't know how long he waits.

Two officers climb from the car. He watches them press buttons on the radios pinned to their chests and he doesn't remember their names even though they're written on their shoulders.

'She was right here,' Noah points to the chairs where they sat a few hours before. 'I went inside and when I came back she'd gone.' When he speaks the words taste of iron and salt: a clenched jaw and bleeding gums.

Another police car arrives and they begin to check each room while he's carefully watched at the kitchen table.

'I'll take the loft,' says one of them who wears perfume that's too strong for this late at night. He hears the thud of the hatch being pushed out and ladders being extended. He begins to think of ropes and wooden beams and is glad when she returns with a shaking head.

'Clear,' she says.

It's beginning to get light outside and they start to search the garden. He wants to say to them that they need to be out there, wherever there was, looking for her: she isn't here hidden in the back garden. He knows this: he'd already checked. He watches them look for patches of disturbed earth and soil on the tyres of his car. They unlock the shed, unroll the tarpaulin that is stored there and check it. His neck aches and although he hasn't smoked for years, he craves a cigarette. Soon one of the police officers is knocking on his neighbour's doors. He sees him asking questions and taking notes.

'Is there anyone who can come and stay with you?' the other officer asks.

'No,' he says, 'my family live hours away.'

'Okay,' she says and Noah notices that she doesn't know what to do with her hands. She catches his eye and then slides them between her stab-vest and t-shirt. He thinks of how she would be able to feel her collarbone beneath the material of her uniform.

'No, there's no-one.' He hears his voice as he says this and he thinks of broken things.

Three weeks pass and then four and each day he's more sure she isn't coming back. Every night he wakes up sweating and thirsty. His dreams are too bright and too hot and he remembers them too clearly. He wonders if he should go back to work: the messages are less frequent and less sorry and he can take as long as he needs but unfortunately the time off can't be paid any more.

It's a Tuesday morning when he sees the police officer at his front door. It was the one who'd climbed into his loft. He remembered now that he'd heard her coughing as she'd come down the stepladder and then the stairs and that there were tangles of spider web on her black sleeves when she'd come back into the kitchen. He hadn't noticed at the time and he wonders about all the other things he hadn't noticed or that he'd forgotten about. He looks at her face and he sees bad news.

'We know where Adel is,' she says, 'and we know she doesn't want to come home.' There's a disturbance in his lungs: something violent takes away his breath. This is not what he thought she'd say.

'She's called us. She wants you to know that she's safe and that she's sorry.'

The police officer doesn't meet his eyes when she says this and he watches her run her fingertips along the side of her neck.

'There's nothing else I can tell you,' she says and then, like before, 'is there anyone I can call to come and stay with you?'

'No,' he says and he notices that the tick of the clock seems louder now. The front door closes with a faint click and he hears the gravel under her boots as she walks away.

He wonders how Adel left so silently. He wonders if there were times when she'd tried to talk her way out of his life or if this was the first time she'd wanted to go and so she'd gone.

Bees

The schools have broken up for summer now and children play behind the fences of hot front gardens. On Lorne Street there's a house with pink and yellow roses. The petals feel like wax between your fingers and they're cool when you press your nose into the flowers. There are lavender plants too: they're thick and silver and they grow all along the fence. Stems have pushed through the gaps in the wood and their purple flowers brush the pavement. Amber had meant to cut them back but now it seems a shame because the flowers are so pretty and the bush is always full of bees.

When she was small Amber learnt that there are over 250 kinds of wild bee. She knows that there are also 225 different kinds of solitary bee and that these are her favourite. Solitary bees have small, narrow bodies and orange fur around their heads. There is a part of them that looks like a neck and this is covered in fur too. She never could remember the name for that part. She thinks it looks as though they have manes and sometimes she wonders what kind of world it would be if bees could roar.

The solitary bee lives alone and chooses holes in the ground, sandy banks and crumbling mortar to make its home. There are probably some nesting in the walls of Amber's house, high up and deep inside the brick. She can't help but wonder why, when there are so many others like them, they would choose to live alone this way.

It's just after 11 o'clock and Amber can feel the heat building already. The children are outside playing on the grass. She can hear their voices through the open window and the wheels of their toy prams across the path in the front garden. Her desk is beneath the bay window and when she stands she can see them in the garden as they play. They are five now, Jasmine and Jade, and Amber can't decide if the time goes fast or slow.

Today Amber is drawing in pencil and she's making sketches for a children's book. The book is about holidays and adventure and flying kites on a beach. She doesn't write the stories: she draws the pictures. Today she draws a boy in blue dungarees with orange hair. He has his arm stretched towards the sky, but at the moment his hand is empty. The paper she's using is thin and, in the breeze from the window, it lifts and curls at the corners.

Later, her back begins to ache. She stands and sees the girls playing on the grass. The front door is open and they've wheeled prams full of dolls and bats and balls out into the garden. They're playing catch and kicking a burst tennis ball. Ashley from two doors down is in the garden too. This was okay, he'd been told by his dad, as long as he shut the gate behind him. The girls weren't allowed to cross the road, but they could visit Ashley's garden as long as they all held hands when they walked there and they told Amber that they were going first.

The sun is hot and bright: it's lunch time and she should make them something to eat. Amber stands and stretches. The boy on the page has string in his hand now and the kite is high above him. The beach is empty and she thinks he looks lonely. Later she will add people to the background. They will watch him as he flies the kite and they will smile and shout to him as he twists and pulls it through the air. The balls of her bare feet sink into the carpet as she walks and it feels nice between her toes. Downstairs, in the hallway, the open door frames the blue sky and hot light of the sun. In the doorway she shouts:

'It's lunchtime, girls and boys, I'll make sandwiches.'

'Okay,' they say but nobody wants to come inside.

They sit in a circle on the grass. It feels scorched and dry beneath them. They have cheese sandwiches on white bread with pickle. In the middle of the circle is a plate with black grapes and biscuits iced in pink and yellow. The icing crumbles in their mouths as they bite the biscuits and Amber leaves it on her tongue until the coloured sugar has dissolved. They each have a plastic cup that's covered in flowers. There's orange squash inside and ice cubes that are beginning to melt. She wonders if they will remember this day when they are bigger and, if they do, what they will think.

After they've eaten Amber fetches a bottle of sun cream from the fridge. She gets Jasmine first and checks her skin. It's hot but it's still white and clear and it isn't burning. Amber squeezes the cream into the palm of her hand. It feels cold from the fridge. Jasmine squeals and laughs as Amber rubs it over Jasmine's pale arms. The cream is sticky and thick and, when Jasmine's covered, Amber lets her go.

'Your turn, Jade,' says Amber. Jade is standing close to the lavender bush with Ashley and they're both looking towards the ground. Ashley is more tanned than the girls and Amber thinks that he looks like his father, Luther. They moved in to the street about six months ago and she liked Luther right from the start. It was nice to have a good-looking man around again, even if it was down the road as opposed to in the house. And it was especially nice to have one who was so friendly and keen to help out with the kids.

'What are you both looking at?' she said.

'This,' said Ashley. There's a child's cricket bat in his hand and he points the yellow plastic towards a spot on the ground. Amber stands and walks across the grass. Her feet are still bare. She can smell the lavender as she inhales and it's sweet.

There's a pool of shade beneath where the lavender bushes hang across the grass. She kneels down. Soon she sees what they're looking at. There's a bee lying on its back. Every few seconds its legs kick and she hears its quiet buzzing.

'It can't get up,' says Jade.

'No,' says Amber, 'we'll try and help it shall we?' She doesn't wait for the children to answer. She picks up a broken stem of lavender and gently pushes the bee onto its front. For a few seconds she waits but the bee doesn't move.

'It's dead,' says Jasmine and Amber shakes her head.

'Maybe just tired,' says Amber, 'maybe we can help it. Wait here and don't touch.'

The honey is clear and golden. Amber puts two fingers into the jar and pulls them out, sticky and wet. This will be enough. She puts the jar onto the sideboard and goes back outside. Gently she picks up the bee and places it on to the hand that's covered with honey. She hopes it won't sting her and for a few seconds they wait. Soon the bee moves towards the sticky liquid and then it sucks at the honey.

'What's going on, everyone?' says a voice at the gate. They all look up and see Ashley's father.

'Luther, hi,' says Amber, 'we're just saving a bee from exhaustion and certain death.' She laughs and he smiles and she thinks that he has lovely teeth. 'It's a busy time of year for them and sometimes they die from working too hard. Usually a bit of honey or sugar does the trick.' They watch as the bee's wings begin to flutter and then it flies away.

'We saved it,' says Jade and then she picks up her doll and sits on the doorstep.

'You sure did,' says Luther, 'Come on Ash, it's time to go home.'

'I'll just be working upstairs so he's no trouble at all if he wants to stay,' says Amber. She sees Luther's eyes move across her face and down her neck. For a second there's a pause and she feels her cheeks turn hot. He smiles.

'No, we're off to see our friends this afternoon, but thanks so much for the offer, Amber, it's really nice of you.'

'Okay,' she says, 'maybe we'll see you tomorrow.'

'I hope so,' he says and then he smiles again and this time holds her gaze.

'Bye,' says Ashley and Amber watches them as they wave and walk along the street to their house.

There's colour in the sketch now: there's yellow sand, purple shells at the edge of the sea and a red kite in the sky. There are more people too, in green t-shirts with shorts to their knees. Today has been a good day, she thinks. Later, she'll start to work on the next page. There will be ice cream in that one and after that, a boat.

The scream is high-pitched. It lasts for a few seconds and Amber jumps from her chair: it's one of the children. She doesn't stop to look out of the window first. Instead she runs down the stairs, missing the last few steps and stumbling through the hallway and out of the front door. Her foot lands on a shard of broken glass on the path and it cuts her but she doesn't notice yet. She sees that it's Jade who's screaming and she runs to her.

'What is it?' she shouts. But before they answer she knows. Jade holds out her hand and on the fleshy part of her palm she sees the red mark and black sting still in the skin.

'She was trying to save the bees,' says Jasmine. Amber notices the broken jar of honey on the garden path then and the wasps crawling in the thick, sticky syrup.

'Come inside,' she says, 'and I'll make it better for you.' She picks Jade up and carries her into the house. 'Jasmine, you come too.'

The kitchen seems dark for a second and it takes a few moments for Amber's eyes to adjust. She sits Jade on the sideboard. She will have to pull the sting out. She wonders what she will use and she knows that Jade will probably scream again. Amber fetches vinegar from the cupboard. She pours the brown liquid onto a tea towel and presses it onto Jade's hand. The vinegar is strong and it catches at the back of her throat.

Amber hasn't noticed yet, but Jasmine is still outside. Ashley's dad heard the screams: he's standing at the gate now and he's asking if everything is okay.

'Yes,' says Jasmine, 'mum is inside making Jade feel better.'

'That's good,' says Luther, 'I'm sure she'll be mended in no time.' He opens the gate and holds out his hand. 'Are you coming? Ashley is in the car already, we have sweets to share.'

'I'll get my shoes,' says Jasmine and she begins to run towards the house.

'No, no,' says Luther, 'I can carry you. Come on, otherwise Ashley will have eaten them all.' He holds out his hand again and Jasmine walks to him. Dry grass prickles the soles of her bare feet. Luther picks her up.

Ashley is not inside the car and Jasmine can't see where the sweets are. As Luther pulls away from the kerb his palms are sweating. They slide across the steering wheel. He focusses on the road ahead and wonders how many minutes he has before Amber notices that Jasmine is gone.

Ragdoll

The sun is high and there are no clouds in the bright blue sky. The path is winding, dusty and stretches away from the tourist complex.

'Look at that,' says Zack, and he gestures upwards, 'there's not a single cloud. Have you ever seen a sky like that?'

'Maybe once or twice,' says Daisy, 'if I was lucky on holiday. But never in Greece, as I've never been here before.' Zack laughs.

'It's so hot though isn't it?' he says, 'I hope it's not too far to the village. Max will want to eat soon.' He looks beneath the hood of the pram. It's amazing how often a tiny two-year-old needs to eat, he thinks. Max is asleep and holds the arm of his ragdoll tightly in his hand.

'The guy from the pool said it wasn't far, didn't he?' says Daisy. 'I'm sure it's not.' They're walking slowly, relaxed. It's the third day of their holiday and they're finally losing the tension they'd had at home. Daisy remembers the man from the pool earlier that morning, his perfect white teeth when he smiled, how he spoke to Max and made him laugh. The pushchair wheels crunch over the grit of the road and their feet fling dust into the air as they walk.

Fig trees line the side of the road. The leaves are wide and a dark green that looks out of place in the surrounding dust.

'Wasps are the only insect that can pollinate figs, you know,' says Zack. He reaches his hand between the green leaves and pulls a fig from the branch. 'Would you like to share?' he asks. The fig is bulbous, dark, lined. She shivers at the thought that there may be a wasp inside.

'No, thanks,' she says, 'you have it.' Zack shrugs, splits the fruit with his fingers and puts some of the soft flesh into his mouth.

'Sweet,' he says.

'How long have we been walking for now?' asks Zack. The road is uphill, the town much further than they thought.

'Forty minutes, I think.' Max has started to cry: he's hungry and hot beneath the red hood of the pushchair.

'Maybe we should go back to the hotel?' says Zack. 'We can go for a swim and get a beer.'

'Surely we're nearly there now,' says Daisy, 'and won't it be nice to meet some locals. You know, rather than the other Brits around the pool.'

'I don't really care,' he says. He's beginning to look red in the face now. Sweat shines on his forehead, drips down his nose. Daisy notices he's beginning to limp, thinks there must be blisters on his feet.

'Look,' says Daisy, 'cherries.' She picks a few from the tree. They are red-black ripe and soft in her hands. She stands still for a moment. There are tiny birds perched on the branches, pulling at the fat fruit. Their yellow beaks are covered with dark stains. Daisy watches them eat and then fly into the sky when they're full. How nice, she thinks, to be so close to that beautiful blue. She offers a cherry to Zack, holding the fruit in front of him. He pretends he hasn't seen. Daisy puts one in her mouth and the flesh is sweet.

The village is all white walls and cobbled streets. As they pass the houses on the outskirts, there's some shade and they're glad. It's busy here. Daisy thinks that she recognises people from the hotel, but she can't be sure.

Soon, they find a café. There are tables outside and they sit down.

'It's like a postcard,' says Daisy. Wisteria arcs around doorframes and covers the front of white stone buildings. Daisy has Max in her arms now and takes him to look more closely at the plant. He holds his hands towards the purple flowers. These are for me, he is saying, I want them.

'No,' says Daisy and she doesn't let him pull the flowers from the branches.

Max squeals and for a second there's silence as people stop talking and watch her. 'Shhh,' she says, 'come on let's get you something cool to drink.'

Daisy walks back to the table and sits down. She has a headache because of the heat and Max is still squealing, making noises as if he's been pinched or worse. She feels the weight of his small body, the heat from him and how his skin is sticky from the sun cream she'd rubbed over him this morning.

They order water and two glasses of beer, some juice for Max. The waitress is tanned and she's wearing pink lipstick. Zack watches her from over the top of his menu. The waitress knows this and deliberately avoids his eye.

'Here, you take Max,' says Daisy. She passes him across the table and begins to feel the heat of his small body dissipate from her lap. She lights a cigarette. Max wriggles to get down and she watches as Zack holds him tighter against him.

'Put him on the floor,' she says, 'there's nothing here that'll hurt.' The decking beneath them is smooth and clean. He puts Max on to the floor, close to his legs.

'There you go,' he says, 'you can play now.' The waitress brings their drinks. The glasses are cold, taken from the fridge and the beer is colder still. They drink it quickly and order another. Zack finds his book from the basket beneath the pram and begins to read.

'This is more like it,' he says.

'I'll be back in a few minutes,' says Daisy. 'I'm going to find the toilets.'

'Okay,' says Zack without looking up from his book.

Inside the café it's hot, even though the sun doesn't shine in through any of the windows. How can it be this hot in the shade, she wonders. It's relentless. The café is full inside: people avoiding the sun, hoping for air conditioning that isn't there. She follows signs that direct her to the back of the café and through a door to a courtyard. Outside she sees a cat lying in the shade. It has grey, thick fur. Daisy can see the glassy eyes of the animal follow her as she walks. As she nears the far side of the courtyard it stands and walks towards her. It stops and brushes against her bare legs. The cat feels soft and thin beneath the fur. She wonders if it has fleas and thinks of its sharp teeth. She doesn't bend down to stroke it.

'Where is he?' asks Daisy when she arrives back to the table, back to Zack, back to an empty floor. Zack looks up from his book.

'What?' he says, 'he's here isn't he?' He looks beneath the table, notices the blisters on his bare feet. Max is gone: the space empty aside from his ragdoll lying on the floor. Zack picks up the doll, looks around them. The table behind is empty now. Who sat there before? Had there been a family? Or was it a man, on his own, wearing something dark? Zack stands. Daisy is pacing the length of the decking at the front of the café, checking beneath tables, behind burnt legs wearing shorts.

'I'll check inside,' he says, 'he can't have wandered far, can he?' And he couldn't have, could he? But still, there's a tightening in Zack's throat, across his bare, sunburnt shoulders.

'I've just come through that way,' says Daisy, 'he wasn't in there.' She snatches the ragdoll from his hands.

'But you weren't looking for him,' says Zack. 'He's small, and they're easy to miss when you're not looking for them aren't they?' He tries to laugh but it gets stuck and doesn't make it past his lips.

'Fine, you go that way,' says Daisy and gestures towards the door. 'I'm going to check out here. We're right on the road, Zack, what if he's gone in that direction? Fucking hell, why weren't you watching him?'

Inside people turn to look at Zack as he enters. He's trying to be calm. It's still early on. There's still time to find him; they don't need to panic yet, do they? He registers the concern of the family by the door. They must have heard the conversation outside. Soon, people are standing, looking beneath tables, moving chairs, heading out the back entrance to the cobbled courtyard. A few women have gone out front to find Daisy. He hears their feet as they walk quickly across the wooden boards and then on the dusty road in front.

Daisy is shouting Max's name now. Zack can hear her calling and wonders how far away she is. Her voice is high and tight. He hears it shake, he hears it grow louder, higher, reach further across the village. He sees people step from their front doors, into the street, and listen to his wife with open mouths and wide eyes. What they can hear now, is less like words: less human than when she first began to shout.

The police are formal. The man asks questions carefully, the woman sits silently, takes notes. Where did you look, they ask. Did they recognise anyone nearby? Why hadn't they been watching Max? How long was the boy missing before they asked someone to call the police? There's a fan on the table and it makes a noise as it moves. It reminds Daisy of last summer, when a dragonfly was trapped in the kitchen, the sound its wings made against the windowpane.

They write Max's details onto forms, enter him into computer screens. His age is noted (two), his hair colour (blonde), the colour of his eyes (green), the clothes he was wearing (blue shorts, red t-shirt, a white sun hat, silver jelly shoes). Any distinguishing features? Yes, they say, a small birthmark on his neck. All of these things, him in small pieces, thinks Daisy.

The policeman's hair is silver at the temples. He's thin, tense. Daisy can see the ripples of tendon at the base of his neck as he speaks. She tries to concentrate on that, tries to avoid the hard stares of the policewoman opposite her, tries not to think of the weightlessness on her lap, the lack of heat there.

'Why are you not out there looking for him?' asks Daisy.

'There's a process of dealing with these things,' says the man, 'There is a way.' It doesn't sound right, how he says it, but his English is better than their Greek. He stands with his notebook and closes the door of the interview room behind him. The woman doesn't stand. Instead she pulls her chair closer to the desk, watches them closely, watches them as if they are about to make another mistake.

Today they're digging for Max. In the village where Max was last seen there's a patch of earth that's *of interest*. The police had hesitated when they'd said this, when they'd arrived at the hotel to advise a dig was taking place later that day.

Daisy and Zack stand and watch them. They're behind a cordon. Like cattle in a pen, says Daisy. In front of them, pieces of string have been placed on the ground: guides along the earth. A woman in a white suit points at intersecting lines and directs others with spades to begin.

They cut and dig into the soil with precision. Zack is holding Daisy's hand. Or maybe she's holding his. And then somebody is holding her and Zack up.

Soon they pull a long piece of cloth from the earth. And then Daisy falls through the arms of the person trying to keep her on her feet.

The people digging lie the dusty white dress on the floor. It's covered with small blue flowers and there's a pocket on the chest. They put it into a clear plastic bag and it's labelled and taken away. Nobody knows who the dress belongs to. Nobody knows why it was there. Zack wonders who would bury a child's dress like that, wonders why nobody wants to talk about it.

Daisy is crying now. She presses Max's ragdoll to her nose and her tears disappear into the soft material of the doll.

Seven months later Daisy is at home. Zack isn't there any more because she made him leave. In her bed there's no room for him now: the ragdoll sleeps on his pillow. Today she's changing the sheets. She smooths them and folds them and tucks them in tight at the corners. She plumps her pillows, feels the feathers move inside the case. Isn't it sad that they're no longer attached to birds, that they're no longer in the sky, she thinks, and she wonders if these birds ever even got to fly.

Jessica

It was nine pm and of course he was on time. He'd said that he would be and he didn't disappoint her. She'd been ready for an hour, although she'd still been looking in the mirror, minutely altering her reflection with powder and lipstick at five minutes to. Her hair was loose and curly. Usually she tied it up but she thought he might like it like this. There were deliberate dark smudges beneath her eyes, drawn with a pencil, and light pink across her lips. Yes, she looked good.

She saw his car parked beneath the trees across the road. She tapped the glass of the bedroom window lightly with her finger. She knew he wouldn't hear, that he was too far away, but she tapped anyway, willing him to look up. She wanted him to see her illuminated and bright through the darkness outside. Didn't things like that happen in films?

She saw him sit forward and look up. Maybe he saw the movement of her shadow and how it fell onto the patch of lit up grass in the front garden? He raised his hand in a sort of wave and then he sat back so she couldn't see his face again.

The front door closed with a bang and the glass shook. She hadn't meant to pull it so hard. People downstairs would hear as she left. No doubt someone would mention it and give her a hard time in the morning. Well, she'd deal with that tomorrow.

It was Autumn now and much cooler than it had been even a week before. Maybe the skirt and thin jacket had been a mistake. She felt the hairs on her arms rise as she walked across the damp grass to his car. Never mind, it was too late now and his car would be warm. He was bound to have the heater on and she'd bet it was a good one: the car looked quite new. She wasn't sure what he did – they'd only met briefly once before, but it looked like he did okay. His shoes were smart and new too. Her grandma had always said you could judge a man by his shoes.

She was close to the car now. The engine hummed. The bonnet felt warm beneath her fingers as she traced them along the metal. She walked slowly, deliberately as she did this, making sure his eyes followed her through the windscreen and watched as she climbed into the passenger seat.

'Wow,' he said, 'don't you scrub up well?'

'Thanks,' she said, 'a bit different from the first time we met isn't it.'

Mark winked. 'I guess nobody ever gets dressed up to go to the corner shop do they? Still, even then I thought you were stunning.' She blushed and looked out of the window so he couldn't see. 'Here,' he said, 'these are for you.' She turned back towards him and he handed over the gifts. There was a single red rose wrapped in cellophane and a bottle of pink wine. 'That's what you drink, isn't it?' he asked.

'You should know,' she said, 'you're the one who insisted on buying it for me when we met.'

'I couldn't let a damsel in distress go without her wine now, could I?' He smiled and she saw a gap in his mouth where there was a tooth missing. She wondered how he'd lost it but she didn't ask.

'No,' she said, 'I was only ten pence short as well, you'd have thought he'd have let me off.' Mark laughed.

'Well, I'm, sure that wasn't the only reason.' Her face feels hot again and she looks away. 'I mean, you were already quite drunk – he probably didn't want to encourage you.'

'It was a Saturday night,' she said, 'and he doesn't usually have a problem. I'm a regular customer there.'

'Very loyal. You are a good girl aren't you,' he laughed.

'Only when it's necessary,' she said.

'Oh, I like the sound of that,' he said, 'now, where to? I was thinking a pizza and then we can share that wine. What do you reckon?'

'Why not,' she said, 'I don't have anything better to do.' He looked at her and then they laughed and the car pulled away from the kerb.

'Have you been here before?' he asked.

'No,' she said, 'never.'

'I love it. Especially when it's dark. Just look at that view.' He moved his hand, palm up and gestured towards the outside. Through the windscreen they could see the lights of the city in front of them. The car was parked on a hill and behind them were fields of grass, wildflowers, a few trees. Mark picked up another slice of pizza from the box. 'It's a special place, I think.'

'Yeah, it's nice,' said Jessica. The clasp of her bra dug into her spine. It was new and she wriggled to move the tight elastic across her back.

'Feel free to take it off if you'd be more comfortable,' Mark said, 'you can give it to me if you like.' He raised his eyebrow, held out his hand and she saw the blue veins on his soft wrists.

'No, it's fine,' she said through a mouthful of pizza. And she wanted to laugh but it didn't feel quite right. She picked up the bottle of wine, drank. Her fingers were greasy and she left smudges on the glass.

'So, can I give you a kiss yet?' asked Mark, 'I've been trying to be a gentleman but I can't wait any longer.' Jessica inhaled to talk but choked on the wine in her mouth. Mark laughed.

'Sorry, I didn't mean to scare you.'

'Why would you think I'm scared?' she asked. Mark tilted his head towards her.

'No reason at all,' he said.

His lips were warm. She could smell the cheese from the pizza as they kissed and she hoped that her breath was sweet from the wine. His hand was on her thigh. Her legs looked pale in the light of the moon. She wondered if she should push her tongue into his mouth or if this was something he preferred to do to her.

Later Mark said that it was time they got back – it was a school night after all and they didn't want to get into trouble. Jessica laughed.

'You've not actually said what you do,' she said.

'That's because it's boring and we had much more interesting things to talk about,' he said.

'Oh go on, give me a clue at least,' she said.

'Okay, if you insist. I run my own business,' he said, 'mostly I buy and sell: cars, phones, that kind of thing. But I go after whatever I can make money from, really.' He paused to see if she was looking at him. She was and so he carried on. 'See, I told you it was boring, didn't I? Still, it pays the bills and means I can treat beautiful women like you to a pizza every now and then.'

Jessica laughed. The wine had gone to her head. She turned the radio up as they drove and she moved her bare shoulders in time to the music. His hand was still on her thigh and the heat from his palm felt good.

'Fuck.' The alarm was ringing, it was 7am. She opened one eye and pressed the off button. What was she thinking staying out when she had to be up so early? She'd sleep in a bit longer: she turned over, closed her eyes again.

She couldn't help but smile as she pulled on her uniform. She could still smell his aftershave on her skin. It was 8.45 when she stood at the front door. She'd be late now, but fuck it, it was worth it. Her head ached from the wine the night before but there was a flutter in her stomach.

'Morning,' said Jemima from downstairs, 'that was some slam of the door as you left last night.'

'It just got caught by the wind,' said Jessica. 'I'll try and keep it down next time.'

'Well, you were much quieter when you got back. Quite lucky really considering how late it was. Who were you out with?'

'I really don't think that's anything to do with you, Jemima. Now, if you don't mind, I'm going because I'm already late.' Seriously, who did that woman think she was? It had started to rain. Jessica pulled up her hood and ran to the bus stop.

She saw his car as she turned the corner of the street. Was it? Yes it was, that was where he'd parked last time. He must've have liked it beneath the trees.

'Hello,' she said. His window was already open – he must have seen her approaching in his mirror.

'Hello,' he said, 'good day at the office?'

'Just the usual,' she laughed, 'so what are you doing here?'

'I've come to see you,' he said, 'I had such a lovely time last night. I wanted to come and say thank you. And also to give you this.' He handed her a box wrapped in silver paper.

'What is it?' she asked.

'Open it and you'll find out,' he said. The paper tore easily. Beneath the silver she saw a mobile phone box. 'Well, what do you think?' He held her eyes until she looked down towards the package in her right palm.

'It's really nice of you, but I already have a phone,' she said.

'I know that, silly. But I noticed the other night that yours has a crack across the screen.'

'Yes,' she said, 'but it's only a small crack. It still works perfectly fine.' She looked at him with a question on her face.

'I'm sure it does,' he said, 'but please, take it. It's a gift and a thank you.' He smiled but didn't show his teeth. She thought he looked embarrassed and so she leant forwards, closer to him in the car. Its engine was still running.

'Thank you,' she said, 'I love it.' He looked her up and down, his eyes settling on her chest for a second.

'Aren't I good to you?' he said, 'now come closer and give me a kiss.'

She kissed his mouth and he smelt of aftershave and soap.

'So how about I pick you up later? I thought you might like a sleepover at mine?' He smiled and there was that gap in his teeth again. She kind of liked it.

'Yes,' she said, 'I'll see you later.'

It was 10am when she pushed open the front door. Jemima was in the hallway. She looked worried. Jessica hated that look of false concern she had. It was so obvious she just wanted to know what she'd been up to.

'Are you okay, Jessica?' she asked, 'it's not like you to stay out all night. I was getting worried.'

'I'm fine,' said Jessica. She was tired, didn't have the stomach for questions this morning. There had been a lot of wine drinking last night. Jemima was standing in front of her. 'You don't even know me, Jemima, now get out of my way – I need to get by.'

'There's no need to be so rude, Jess, but I suppose you do have somewhere to be. It is a weekday after all.'

'You look great,' he said as she closed the car door. 'I'm so lucky. I've been telling my friends all about you, you know.' She smiled.

'Yes, so where are you taking me tonight?'

'Well, I thought as it was a Saturday and neither of us has to be up tomorrow, we could go and party. A few friends are having drinks and I thought it was about time I introduced you.'

'Sounds good,' she said.

'And look,' he said gesturing to the back seat, 'I've got you that pink wine you love.'

After forty minutes Mark stopped the car. *Banbury Road.* The house was neat from the outside. The front lawn tidy, trimmed. There were shiny cars on the driveway.

'Detached,' she said, 'this looks nice.'

'I know,' he said, 'I know all the best people,' and he squeezed her hand. 'You look beautiful tonight, Jess.' He whispered in her ear and his breath was wet, hot. 'Are you coming in? There's no need to be shy - they're dying to meet you.'

Of course she'd been to parties before. There had always been lots of drinking.

But the cocaine was new: she'd never taken cocaine before. Her friends didn't have the money for this kind of thing.

It was strange at first. But then good and she liked it.

Mark had a lot of friends. There were six men who told her their names and said it was nice to see her. She wasn't good with names, she said, and she forgot them straight away. There were two women but they didn't speak much. They wore lots of makeup and Jess felt like she wasn't wearing enough. There was a lot to drink and then they'd stood in a circle in the kitchen. Someone started to pass around a blue plate and a rolled up fifty. She didn't think she'd ever seen a fifty before.

'Your turn,' said Mark as he'd handed her the plate. 'Don't be shy – none of us are.' He winked and she took it. It was warm in her hands and she hadn't expected that.

It had reminded her of inhaling sherbet when she was small. And it looked pretty much the same. Except it was more white than the powder she'd got with the liquorice. Then she'd wanted to talk and dance and other people were dancing so she'd joined in. Mark handed her a drink and she didn't remember much after that. Except that one of the women held her hair when she was sick. And when she was lying on the bed later on, she heard somebody say that Mark liked them young and then they'd laughed.

There were police cars when they'd turned the corner.

'I wonder what's going on,' said Jessica.

'Do you mind if I drop you here?' asked Mark. 'It's just I've got to get off now. You know how it is.'

'Yeah, of course. I'll see you soon.'

'Without a shadow of a doubt,' he said. This time he didn't kiss her before she climbed from the car; instead he kept his eyes on the road.

Jessica pushed open the front door and braced herself for Jemima and her questions.

'Jess,' she heard her say from the room on the right of the corridor. 'Thank goodness.' She appeared in the doorway. 'Where have you been? We've not seen you for two days.'

'I don't have to answer to you, Jemima, and I'm sick of you keeping tabs on me.' She put her hand on the bannister. She was tired. She just wanted to sleep.

'Jess,' you need to come in here and talk to us,' Jemima gestured towards the room she'd just come from. 'There are people here you need to speak to.'

'No,' said Jessica, 'I'm tired.'

'Jess, please, you're thirteen. The staff here are responsible for you while you're in care. We were worried, we *are* worried. The police are here because we called them. Nobody knew where you were.'

'I knew,' said Jessica, 'and I'm back now and I'm going to bed.'

'I'm sorry,' said Jemima - she was talking to the police officers now – 'we can't force her to talk to us can we?'

Jessica opened her eyes. The curtains of her bedroom weren't drawn but the room was dark. She must've slept for most of the day. She felt warm beneath the duvet and she didn't want to move. Her phone had been ringing: that's what woke her up. But now it had stopped and for a few seconds there was silence. Jessica turned over and picked it up. *Missed call Mark* flashed on screen. She closed her eyes but then the ringing began again. She lifted the phone to her ear.

'Hello.'

'Hello,' said Mark, 'why didn't you answer?'

'I was asleep,' she said, 'you woke me.'

'Well, get dressed, sleeping beauty. I'm coming to pick you up.'

'Actually,' she hesitated, 'I better not tonight. I got a really hard time from Jemima after staying out. The police were here when I got back and were asking questions about where I'd been.'

'You didn't tell them about me, did you?' he asked. His voice was slow, cool.

'No, I didn't tell them anything,' she said. 'It's none of their business who

I choose to spend time with.'

'Good girl,' said Mark, 'I doubt they'd be interested anyway. It's obviously just Jemima being a bitch. Maybe she needs to get herself a boyfriend and have some fun of her own.'

'Yes,' said Jessica, 'maybe I'll tell her that.' Mark laughed.

'The police have left now, haven't they?'

'Yes,' said Jessica.

'So fuck them. They obviously don't care otherwise they'd still be hanging around. It's lucky you've got me now, isn't it. And we have fun don't we?'

'Yes,' she said, 'but I'm really tired. And there's school tomorrow.'

'One day off won't hurt. Now come on, I have a bottle of your favourite in my car. You know you want to.'

'No,' she said, 'maybe tomorrow instead?'

'Jess,' he said, 'I thought you liked me?'

'I do,' she said.

'Then do as you're told and don't get me all upset. You don't want me to tell Jemima what you've been up to do you? Imagine the lectures and the visits from the police then. You'd be in so much trouble. They'd probably move you somewhere out of the city: somewhere you've never even visited.'

'They wouldn't,' she said. Her voice was quiet now and her face felt hot.

'They would, Jess, I've seen it happen before. Now, you need to get dressed: wear a skirt. I'm on my way over and I've got a friend I want you to meet.' She tried to talk but she couldn't make the sounds. 'Hurry up, Jess, because I won't be long. And the thing is, you kind of owe me.'

Caterpillars

They're laughing. They think it's all a joke. The youngest one is collecting them from the low leaves of trees. She screams when they move in her hand. The older one holds them beneath the water in the bucket with a stick.

They are my children and they're drowning caterpillars. I wonder if they know that these crawling things would've become butterflies.

Soon, the child-minder will be here. Maybe she will tell them. Maybe they will cry.

My bags are already in the car. I have written a note that I will leave by the kettle when I go.

Gone

She had tiny wrists and Lucas wondered how they would feel in his hands. It was some time in the evening and the windows of the bus framed a sky that was low down and dark.

She paid for her ticket and the driver pulled away from the kerb. Lucas watched as she took the printed paper from the machine and screwed it tightly in her palm. Soon she was level with his seat and half fell as the bus turned a corner. The aisle felt narrow and wide at the same time. Lucas watched her eyes pass quickly over his face as she sat down. He knew she didn't really see him, though, and so he looked away.

The road took them out of the city and he watched for a few minutes as buildings began to fall away to fields. The woman had swung her backpack on to the empty place beside her and for a few minutes she was still.

The woman unzipped the rucksack and pulled out a map and pen. She placed them on her lap and then pushed her hand deep inside the bag. She was searching for something and Lucas watched as she pulled jumpers, socks, a shoe into the light and then pushed them back down again.

'Fucking hell,' she said, 'I was sure I had some.' Except she wasn't saying this to anyone and so nobody answered her. She sat back in her seat and Lucas watched as she exhaled all the air from her lungs. As her shoulders fell he wondered how her breath would feel on his face. She pressed her temples with her thumbs and he saw circles of white appear on her skin. He watched her hesitate and then reach out to the man in front of her.

'Sorry,' she said, 'I wonder if you have anything I could take for a headache?' She put her hand on the man's shoulder as she said sorry but then slid it onto the metal of the seat as he tensed and turned his head.

'Pardon,' he said, 'what did you say?'

'I have a headache and I wonder if you might have something I could take? I thought I had some painkillers but I can't find them.' The man had white hair and a shirt that was buttoned tightly across his thick neck.

'No, I don't,' he said and shook his head as if she shouldn't have asked. He turned then and looked towards the front of the bus. She didn't sit back for a few seconds: instead she watched the side of the old man's face. Lucas saw there was a raw line of red skin across the man's jaw. He guessed it was where he'd caught it with a razor that morning.

The woman raised her hand towards the man as if she was going to speak again but instead turned to look at the others on the bus.

Lucas felt her eyes on him and his skin felt hot. It was difficult to speak although he wasn't sure why. Outside the sky had split and bright pieces of snow began to fall. The woman sat back and put her head onto her backpack. The lights on the bus were dim and yellow. She rubbed her eyes. The black mascara from her lashes smudged across her face like marks from a fire. She covered her eyes with a scarf. It was thick and soft and Lucas wanted to touch it.

Lucas picked up his bag and placed it onto his lap. He'd packed just before he left and there were enough clothes for an overnight stay. Ruby had sent him a message to make sure he was on his way. *You'll get the car fixed soon,* she'd written, *and then it won't take you so long to get here.* Except he didn't think he would get the car fixed because he liked the bus ride out of the city. It made him feel like he was going somewhere. Somewhere he'd planned on going when he was younger but just hadn't gotten around to yet. Except he knew he wasn't going to any of those places, not really.

He remembered his friend from school who would ride the bus one way across the city and then back again just for something to do. He'd told Lucas he would sit upstairs so he could look into gardens usually hidden by fences and walls and pretend to be somewhere new.

The weather had been freezing cold for a few days now: much colder than he remembered last winter. The windows were covered in steam. Lucas ran his palm across the glass. He peered through the gap, into the bare fields now bright with snow. The woman with the tiny wrists was asleep. He wondered where she was meant to get off the bus and if she would miss her stop. Except maybe she didn't have a stop. Maybe she made it up as she went along and she'd get off where she woke up.

Lucas had often seen people with backpacks out here. The countryside was beautiful even in winter. He knew of at least one hostel this way. He'd heard people talking of it before, though he wasn't sure which unmarked, dirt road it would be at the end of.

Would the woman know? He imagined she might have it circled on the map she had in her lap. Or maybe not and she was just guessing. He wondered if the fear of not knowing added something to the journey when you travelled.

There were hills outside now, that met the horizon, and he knew they carried on beyond where he could see. The smallness of his life frightened him. He always felt like this when there were hills or mountains or sea that touched the sky. He mattered to Ruby. But if he left she'd only miss the parts of him that he worked hard to make her like, the parts of him he wasn't even sure were real.

Once, he wrote a list of things he would take if he left and got a rucksack from a shop that sold walking boots and tents. That was years ago. Ruby said he was too old to go travelling now. She said it was something that kids did and that he was too late. She said he'd just have to stay lost for the rest of his life, and then she'd laughed, and said at least he'd been lucky to find her and maybe he should just be thankful for that. He'd nodded his head.

Lucas noticed the woman's eyes moving beneath her lids. He wondered what she was dreaming about. Some mornings he would keep his eyes closed after waking to stop his dreams from escaping. It was something he'd done from childhood. It never worked and they always faded, but still, it was a habit he couldn't lose.

He put his hand on his thigh and felt the plastic blisters of a packet in his pocket. These were on prescription for the migraines that used to come every week. Recently they weren't so often, but he still visited the doctor for new pills to swallow. He took them with beer on the nights he didn't work and during the days when there was nothing to do with his hands. The drugs blurred the edges of the evenings so they passed in a way he didn't mind as much.

They were becoming a habit, something he sometimes worried about but he did it anyway, didn't really want to stop. Ruby hadn't noticed yet but he knew that she would. He worked so hard to be good to her, to conjure love because he knew she was a good woman. He wanted it to be enough.

Too much time had passed now and he was embarrassed to offer the pills to the woman with the backpack. She was awake and had wound the scarf around her neck. The woman picked up the heavy rucksack and stood. Then she pressed the bell and seconds later the bus stopped.

Through the glass Lucas watched as she opened the map and began to trace it with her fingertips. The noise of the engine rose again, the bus pulled forward, frozen white fields slid across the windows. Lucas placed his hand on to the seat beside him and felt the coolness of the material. Then he stood and ran to the front of the bus.

'I need to get off,' he shouted. The driver hesitated and then pressed the brake.

It was dark on the lane and his eyes took a few seconds to adjust.

'Hello,' he shouted, 'are you there? I have something for your headache.' He shouted again but louder this time, 'Hello,' and his heart pushed against his ribs, 'Are you there?' But there was no answer because the woman had gone, and now nothing would be different.

Strawberry Fields

There's a photograph of Finn from that day. She's kneeling between long rows of green leaves and the low dark bushes hide hearts of red fruit. James keeps it in his wallet.

It was Finn's birthday and she was turning four. They'd thought it would be nice to leave the city for a while: to find green spaces that didn't hide broken glass, barbs of beer cans shredded by mowers. It was Eve's idea. There was a farm eight miles out of the city and you could see the sign for *Anderson's Strawberry Farm* from the road. A tall board with a painted red fruit showed you the way.

'I'll drive,' Eve had said. She preferred it that way. She liked to know where she was going and how she was going to get there. James was in the passenger seat, packed in with bags of juice and sandwiches. They'd invited seven children and a convoy of cars followed the winding road. Finn was in the back and quieter now they were out of the city. There wasn't the stop-start at traffic lights, and the winding of the bends lulled them to a temporary silence.

There was a pub next door to Anderson's. They'd visited a few weeks before because of a diversion on the motorway. They heard on the traffic news that people had died. It'd taken ages to move the mash of metal and flesh from the road. They noticed the pub as they twisted along back roads, following the diversion's yellow triangles. Eve had slowed the car and they'd stopped and gone inside for a drink.

It was warm when they went inside and the ceiling was low. There was a drunk at the bar and he watched them as they walked through the door. The seats were covered with faded velour and dark heavy curtains were draped across the tiny window. The drunk was slurring words across the room and the man serving tried not to listen. Then he ordered another whiskey, on the slate please and thanks Rod I'll sort you out soon. James thought there was a flash of recognition across Eve's face. But she said no, James, how would I know him? And how would she. The drunk was saying something they couldn't hear now and he smiled as he said it. They both stopped talking after that and finished what was in their glasses.

Back in the car Eve saw the sign for the farm. She decided they would come back one day in summer when the sun shone and you could smell the fruit from the road as you drove by.

They turned into the driveway of Anderson's Farm. The fields didn't end until they reached the sky and they were the kind of green you'd get in the pages of a book. From the entrance they saw a faded silver barn. They drove towards it and parked.

A man came to greet them.

'Hello,' he said, 'welcome to the strawberry fields.' This must be Anderson thought James. The man gestured somewhere to his left and looked past them as he spoke. 'What a beautiful day you've come to visit us.' He was tall and his skin was dark from the weather. He told them the field behind was for picnics and then he handed over baskets for the fruit they would pick after lunch.

They sat on the grass to eat and as James unwrapped the foil from the sandwiches he could see that there were workers inside the barn. The children were noisy now: excited to find the fruit they'd been promised. The workers were packing strawberries into plastic punnets and sweating because of the heat. The party finished their sandwiches and drank orange juice from cool cartons.

After lunch James pushed open the gate to the strawberry fields and everyone chose a row with their children. Then they were all on their knees pushing and pulling at plant leaves to find the fattest, reddest fruit they could. Some of the children squeezed the strawberries in their hands. They loved the squelch of the pulp in their palms and everybody laughed. Maybe this was how they made jam. The sun shone and they could smell the damp earth from where the plants had been watered early that morning. Some of the children sat among the bushes and it was as if they'd just been delivered by the stork.

Eve walked along the rows of plants, took photographs, got further away. The silver of the camera flashed in the light of the sun: the reflections made rainbows on the soil. Then somebody joked that the country air was getting to him and he needed a cigarette. James turned to him and laughed. It was only a second but when James turned back Eve was gone. Only the camera remained, hung from the gate by its strap. He looked across the surrounding fields but he couldn't see her. James shivered even though the sun burned his neck. It's okay he thought, she's just gone for a walk across the nearby fields.

Half an hour passed and then an hour. People were asking where Eve had gone and wasn't it time to head back now because the children were tired and the invitation said the party was only until three. James told everyone to go home and so they picked up their children and baskets of strawberries and left. He was sure she'd just got distracted wandering in the fields and lost track of time.

An hour and a half after they should've left, Anderson came out of the barn. James told him Eve had disappeared over the fields and that he didn't know what to do now. Anderson said that he would go out and take a few others to look for her. Finn was cold and tired so James wrapped her in a blanket from the car, laid her on to the back seat. He locked the doors and held the keys tightly in his hand.

A while later Anderson came back.

'There's no sign of her,' he said, 'I'm calling the police, because it'll be dark soon.' Seconds later James heard him speaking to his wife on the phone. The wind brought his voice back from where he stood on the driveway. He said that he'd be late because some woman from the city had taken herself off over the fields and got lost. Or something.

There were police then and it was dark. James asked them how a grown woman could disappear when they'd managed to keep hold of all the children.

It's early evening and Finn is in bed now. It's been nine months and Eve's face is becoming more difficult to remember. There are certain parts James can still conjure but he struggles to summon its wholeness. Now he has to hold a photograph: Finn kneels between green rows of leaves searching for hearts of red fruit. Eve stands behind her and looks past the camera into the sunshine. She shades her eyes with her hand and it's like she hasn't noticed James taking the picture at all.

When the Sun Sets

'Jamie, look: any minute now we'll be able to see the sea. Are you ready?'

June is on the back seat of the car with him. Phil is driving. 'Look at how flat everything is,' she says, 'it makes the sky look so big. I've never seen unbroken sky like this anywhere else. I love Norfolk.'

'I know,' says Phil, 'you say that every time we come here. Every year for the past seventeen.' He laughs.

'I know,' June says, 'but it's beautiful. Especially in weather like this. It makes you feel so small doesn't it: lost in a sea of sky.'

'You're such a romantic,' says Phil.

It's a hot day and the windows of the car are rolled down. There are wisps of white cloud and fields of rape glow yellow as far as they can see. The world shimmers in the heat.

'I'm seventeen,' says Jamie.

'I know,' says June. She holds his hand and it's damp. 'We come here every year and the first time we visited was the year you were born.' Jamie looks out of the car window. June tries to follow the line of his eye, to see what he is seeing. 'You remember this scenery don't you,' she says. But Jamie doesn't answer and they listen to the songs on the radio instead.

Soon they pass the sign for Docking. It's a small village with a chip shop and a pub. Wisteria grows around front doors. The post office doesn't have a queue.

'I remember,' says Jamie.

'What do you remember?' asks June.

'Dog,' says Jamie.

'No, there's no dog. But we had lunch at that pub last year. We sat outside in the sun.' There are people outside now: a group of four, all quite young. The women wear sunglasses, light cigarettes and lift their pint glasses to say cheers.

'I think he does remember,' says Phil, 'there was a dog there last time with that family we got talking to. It was a black Labrador.'

'Blue,' says Jamie.

'Yes,' says Phil, 'it was wearing a blue collar.'

'Wow,' says June, 'what a good memory.'

The campsite is set back from the road, hidden by surrounding trees. There's a walk to the beach through the woodland behind them and if they are quiet they can hear the sea.

Phil takes the tent from the boot of the car. The material is faded orange and heavy. Jamie sits on the grass looking at the trees and how they move in the breeze.

'That's home sorted for the next week,' says June, 'now time for a cup of tea, don't you think?' Nobody answers, of course, because it's not a question. She picks up the small cooker from the tent, places it on the grass outside and lights the ring. Purple flames spit from the metal and she puts a silver kettle on the fire.

Later, there's wine. The camp fire glows and crackles in the darkness. The rest of the campsite is quiet and navy blue. June holds Phil's hand. It's warm and soft in her palm. The flames of the fire shrink and grow.

'Shall we go to bed?' asks Phil.

'Yes,' she says, 'yes.' And she thinks of his solid body and how he will hold her.

He can see her white skin through the darkness, feel her ribs and the skin stretched and taut across the bones. He tries to be quiet but his breathing is heavy now. He runs his hands across her stomach, feels the smoothness of her skin and then the scar that's now seventeen years and three months old.

It had started as they'd been told it would. They stayed calm, got to hospital in plenty of time. Had the bag June had carefully packed weeks before.

She'd pushed for hours, done her best, done what she was told. But things were taking too long: there was a problem.

'The cord is wrapped around the baby's neck and his heartbeat has dropped,' said a consultant. 'We need to carry out an emergency caesarean and you have to be sedated for this.' The consultant looked dark under the eyes and her forehead wrinkled when she looked at June.

'Of course,' said June, 'do whatever you need to do.'

It didn't take them long to make the uneven cut and pull the baby boy from her stomach. He was born quickly in the end but he was already blue. They put him in an incubator and the consultant told them that it was probably bad news.

Phil is asleep now, the rhythm of his breath changed. Slowly June opens the compartment of their bedroom. She stands and tiptoes across the ground sheet, feels the flattened grass, the uneven earth beneath her feet. She opens the zip, pulls back the material of the tent that makes Jamie's bedroom. Inside she sees the lines of him through the darkness. His duvet is twisted. Half his body uncovered, his long limbs soft with sleep.

She watches him for a few minutes. She's done this since he was born. In the beginning she would listen for his breath, but now this watching him is just the routine of her life. She kneels, reaches across and pulls the duvet to cover his body. He's so big now: taller than her and lately she has started to worry. It was easy to keep him safe when he was small, when she could put him into a pram and push him around the park.

She closes the zip, crosses the tent and climbs back into her own bed.

It's only nine a.m. but already the beach is busy.

'Everybody gets up so early when they're camping, don't they?' says June. 'Wow,' says Phil, 'today is going to be a scorcher.' They're walking down the steps onto the beach, the sand is soft beneath their feet and it slows their pace.

'Here?' asks June.

'Here,' says Phil and they put down their bags, shake open the towels and lay them on the ground.

June has a book with her, Phil has newspapers and a crossword. Jamie has a bucket and spade. He digs and moves the sand from one area of the beach to another and then back again. He re-seals the holes perfectly, pats them down so you might not know they ever existed. Except the surface is darker, smoother: disturbed in a different way.

The sea is cold when they paddle.

'Wow,' says Phil, 'it'd take your breath away if you went any deeper than your knees.'

'I'm going to try it,' says June. And Phil watches her wade out and then plunge her shoulders beneath the waves. It doesn't take her long to stand up. 'You were right!' she shouts through a deep intake of breath. They laugh and she does it again. 'Jamie are you coming?'

He's standing in the water and Phil holds his hand. His skin looks pale against his colourful swimming trunks and June notices that he's almost as tall as Phil.

Jamie doesn't move but a wave laps in and hits them higher on their legs. Jamie laughs, lets go of Phil's hand and looks further out to sea.

'You're getting brave these days aren't you? Are you having a lovely time?' shouts June. Jamie doesn't answer but she's sure that he is.

It's early evening now. They finished at the beach a while ago, had fish and chips from the chip shop in Docking.

'It's not even school holidays yet but I can't believe how busy the place is,' says Phil. 'Shall we go back to the beach and watch the sun set? In fact the next beach along will be quieter, let's go there.'

'Yes,' says June, 'that sounds like a lovely idea.'

The car is parked on the quiet road, metres behind them now and they walk along the winding, well-trodden path to the beach. The road turned to sand minutes after they climbed from the car and it feels soft beneath their feet. Phil was right, it is quieter here.

'I bet everyone has gone back to their campsites to get the fires going before it's dark,' says June.

'Or maybe to have dinner,' says Phil, 'but we ate out, didn't we, Jamie? We had fish and chips.' He puts his arm around Jamie's shoulders and squeezes, pulls him tight.

'I can hear the sea now,' says June and as they walk sand banks begin to rise on each side of them. The path is curved and the sea is obscured for the moment. There are hundreds of footprints, maybe thousands, and Jamie bends to touch the shapes in the sand. 'Come on, Jamie,' says June, 'keep up.' They round the corner then and the path opens to a huge, flat beach.

'Wow,' says Phil, 'just look at that. I never get tired of this place.' The beach stretches away to their left and right as far as they can see. In front of them the water doesn't stop until it touches the sky. The sun is beginning to fall now and throws a golden shadow across the water. Phil puts his hands in his pockets, walks down to the water's edge, dips his feet.

'Toilet,' says Jamie.

'Okay,' says June, 'this way.' There's a toilet block back the way they came, a few steps back from the path. She leaves Phil to watch the sun. They'll just be a few minutes and he'll know where they've gone if he turns around.

The toilet block is small. Sand creeps up the steps and on to the concrete floor: remnants of dried footprints. The *Ladies* sign hangs on the left, *Gentlemen* is signed right.

'This way,' says June leading Jamie left.

'No,' says Jamie, 'man,' and he points to his chest. June hesitates, begins to follow but then changes her mind.

'Okay, Jamie, but come back here when you're done,' she says. And Jamie looks at her the way he always does.

June is only gone for a few minutes. She doesn't use the hand drier, doesn't want to miss the sun. She stands outside the toilet block, shakes the water from her palms and wipes her hands across her shorts. She hears the waves crashing on the shore and everything else is silent. A minute passes.

'Jamie?' she shouts, but there's no reply. She passes the *Gentlemen* sign, steps inside. There is nobody at the sinks. She turns, checks the cubicles, finds them all empty.

'Jamie?' she shouts again.

She is back on the path now, looks left, looks right.

'Phil,' she shouts from across the sand. She sees Phil's lone figure, sees the sun lower, closer to the sea. She sees the shadow of evening fall across the ground, sees the empty flat beach and how there is nothing else.

Wasp

Your dad has gone to the chip shop to buy dinner. It's been a long time but he hasn't come back yet. You lean forwards in the car seat, try to see him, search for his face in the street. You cannot find it.

There's a wasp that you do not see. It lands on your shoulder, walks across your spine. You move and it stings you. Startled, you lean back. You squash it and it stings you again.

Your back really hurts. You begin to cry but nobody hears.

The Fox

It's difficult to see where the trees end and the road begins. The sky is dark and the reservoir black. Lorna is crying and she catches her face in the car mirror: it's wet and the salt is beginning to sting. She presses the accelerator harder and the white lines of the road catch in the headlights and disappear beneath the car. There's a solid low-down shadow of something in front of her and she sees its eyes, and they're green. She hears a thud and the sound of something ripped open.

Lorna moves her foot to the brake. She notices the stars crowded in the windscreen and her damp hands slide across the steering wheel. The car stops and behind her she sees the shadow disappear into the woods. She opens the car door and begins to run. The smooth surface of slippery tarmacked road changes to mud and leaves and she runs through trees she does not notice. Fallen branches crack under her feet and she runs until her legs burn and ache. She slows down, walks, stops. She looks around, searches the darkness. There's the smell of wet soil and dying plants and then: something on the floor ahead. She can't make out its edges yet but there's a face through the blackness and she stops running.

The light of a white moon falls through branches overhead. The air beats around her and nothing is still. There's no sound from the shadow on the floor and so she steps closer. She touches it and it doesn't move.

The body is limp in her hands and she can feel it cooling as she begins to pull it along the ground. There are fallen branches and they catch and tear as she tries to move. A thick thread of something wet falls away from the wound on the fox's neck and Lorna is sick beneath the bare branches of an oak tree. She hears the noise of traffic far away and remembers her car left with its doors unlocked and lights still burning by the reservoir. There's a blanket in the boot. She'll leave the fox for now and she'll go back to the car and get it. She'll bring it here to wrap around the body and then it'll be easier to pull the fox through the woods and out to the road. She'll take it home then and bury it beneath the apple tree in her back garden.

She stands up. She's much further from the road than she thought. An owl calls.

The thick weave of the blanket feels coarse between her fingers. Lorna kneels and spreads the material across the floor, close to the fox. She pulls the body towards her and feels the twisted tendons of its legs. She picks up the corners of the blanket and begins to pull. It slides more easily across the wet soil now. The skin of her hands reddens as the blanket rubs. She can't see it in the dark but they throb and her feet slip as she walks.

The moon is lower now. She opens the car door and places the body on to the backseat. Her hands are sticky and she wipes them across her jeans. The reservoir water is still and silver stars sit motionless on the black surface. It's past midnight and the roads are quiet. She'll be home before it's light and she'll bury the fox before her neighbours are awake.

The body is out of the car and blood seeps through the blanket, darkening the grass beneath it. She thinks of black ink and the time she bit a pen until its insides spilled across her tongue and over her chin. It was the night when Adam didn't come home. She'd waited up until the birds had sung and the sky was light. She'd tried to watch television, then she'd listened to the radio and made a list of things to do the day after. She'd thought of calling the police but he was a grown man - it's not like they'd send out a search party for a someone big enough to look after himself. She hadn't noticed the ink until it was too late. The ink was bitter. She'd gagged and ran to spit in to the sink.

He'd arrived home just before 8am and she'd slapped his face as he stood on the doorstep.

'Don't fucking start,' he'd said, 'I was drinking at Jack's and ended up falling asleep on his sofa.' Then he'd pushed past her and climbed the stairs for a shower.

There's a spade propped against the shed. She picks it up and begins to dig. The earth is hard and dry: she shouldn't have chosen here.

It's beginning to get light when she drops the spade to the floor and lights a cigarette. There's a square of dark soil beneath the tree and the earth is mostly level now. The birds are beginning to sing and for a few minutes she's still. There's brandy in the cupboard and she fetches it. It's been ten months and she doesn't wear her wedding ring any more. She watches the birds swoop and pull worms from the freshly turned soil.

The last time she saw him he was standing by the front door. He was wearing his green coat and he zipped it up to the chin. The zip was gold and the coat smelled of wax and damp earth. There was a bag by his feet and he picked it up.

'It's for my camera and flask,' he said, even though she hadn't asked.

'Where are you going?' she said.

'Just to the woods for a walk.'

'Okay, be careful,' she said. And then he smiled and turned away. She remembered the lines around his mouth and the look on his face: how she knew he wasn't coming back and how she was glad.

Robin

It's a hot day and in the garden there is blossom and the sound of birdsong.

She finds it on the grass: its wings fanned at its sides, its chest red fluff. Soon, she notices the parts of it scattered across the ground. She kneels down and sees ropes of tiny, white intestines.

The cat lies in the flowerbeds. It's the fourth bird this week that he's pulled apart for fun. She calls him over and he comes.

There is a spade in her hand and then a thud as the metal connects with the small, hard bones in his skull.

Later, when her girlfriend asks if she's seen the cat, she will say no.

Knowing Something by Heart

It was one day in July and he didn't tell them he was leaving. At a quarter past two in the afternoon he climbed from the window of the classroom and walked across the school fields in the sun. The children in the class watched through the glass as he jumped the fence and ripped his trouser leg. They never saw him again.

The next day the head teacher told them a stand-in would be starting the following week. They finished the school year with a supply teacher whose name none of them would remember.

Mostly it was the look on their faces that he had hated. And the warnings they'd had. They weren't to talk about a missing child. Their teacher would be upset. It had been a year and they still hadn't found her. Everyone knew she'd gone, but nobody seemed to know where.

He started a job in a factory three weeks after he'd left the school. People there called him Tom. Mostly nobody liked to talk. There were no windows and the brick walls were painted white. The electric lights, like fake suns never gave away the time of day. They would reflect on the gloss of the white walls and the wax of the white overalls. Sometimes he thought of clouds and a book he once read about the man that named them.

His wife had left within a year of Iris being lost; she wasn't around to disapprove of his new job. She couldn't look at him any more. She closed the bedroom door on the purple wallpaper and never went in there again. The smell of washing powder and blankets disappeared when the dust came. She said sorry as she left. Because she was. He remembered there was smashed glass on the pavement and it caught the stars.

Sometimes before he fully wakes, these things are unremembered. The morning sky falls through a gap in the curtains. He reaches for his wife, imagines Iris asleep next door. Then there is a burst of something through his brain. The feeling of knowing something by heart creeps back. The house is empty and he remembers.

He can't leave these lonely rooms. One day they might find her: one day they might need to find him.

'And there's the garden,' he said to his mother once. 'It's so beautiful now and it's taken me years.' Mostly the fences are hidden with the white love-heart leaves of ivy. Because the birds love the berries and he likes to watch them. Blossom trees and buddleia burst pink across the sky. Sitting in the garden with a cigarette, he drinks beer and says cheers. But to what he isn't sure.

Iris was playing in the street the day she disappeared. It was Saturday. He wasn't at work. He was in the back garden pulling at weeds and cutting grass. Jenny was washing windows. It was years ago and they hadn't been living there for long. Jenny would watch Iris from the window and that was why she was allowed to play. It was a cul-de-sac and few of them had cars. They didn't need to worry about traffic.

Above the noise of the lawnmower Tom begins to hear Jenny's voice. He quickly switches off the power. He can tell by the tone that he has to hear. That's when she says it. Looking from the window Jenny has realised she can't see her.

'Where is she? Where's Iris?' The wind is loud in his ears now. He walks inside. The mower is still plugged in. The wire trips his feet.

Tom catches his wife as she's running from the front door.

'Where is she?'

'She was here a second ago. We were playing. And then I was skipping. Now I can't see her,' says the girl from next door.

The next thing he remembers is scouring the streets with the neighbours and shouting her name. Later there are police and sirens.

After that they are back at home. The living room is turning cooler now and the curtains are partly drawn. Their faces are in shade but he can still see his wife's swollen eyes. He needs some air.

'I'll go to the shop down the street. We need some milk and there is nothing to eat.' Except he isn't hungry and mostly it's difficult to swallow. The police are still in the house. It's too small for them all and finally they let him go. It's only a short walk. He won't be far. It is early evening and the sun is apple-red in the sky. Blossom foams on the trees. He shivers. There is a cool breeze on his neck when he walks in the shade.

The tins and boxes on the shelves in the shop are a blurred rainbow of colour. He finds the fridge. The glass bottles stand in white formation. He picks one with a silver top. A young security guard walks past. The navy colour of his uniform fills the edge of his right eye. Tom doesn't see him. If he had done, he'd remember the pink cut on his cheek and the blue bruise of his eyelid. It was from a fight the night before. The security guard realised who Tom was when he watched the news the next day. He didn't know where Iris was either.

After three days, the police leave the house. They pack up their cassettes and coats and say they will call should anything change. Then there is nothing.

He still speaks to her. His child. He imagines her face now that she's older and the altered pitch of her voice. All of these missing people; if they go of their own accord, why do they go? And if they're taken, why are they never found?

In the garden he opens a beer. It's July again and the moon is already in the blue sky. He takes a long drink from the can. Pink-footed pigeons catch shards of silver in their wings.

The Ypres Cross

I visit the cathedral every week. I come to see the Ypres cross, to touch the glass that covers it, keeps it safe.

The broken beads wound around the crucifix remind me of the beads my grandmother used to wear. She wore them for special occasions: for nights she wanted to feel beautiful. She looped the string around her throat and they were pale against the dark blue of her blouse.

Next she added colour to her cheeks, lipstick to her mouth. She knew her own face well and did this with precision. Later, she slipped a shawl over her shoulders, stepped out to dance with her friends.

My grandmother doesn't wear her beads any more. She cannot walk, doesn't have the strength to lift her legs. She spends her days in bed now, dying slowly from something they cannot cure.

Sometimes she asks me to put powder across her cheeks, to fetch a mirror so she can see. She tells me how she loves to dance and she asks me for her beads.

When I tell her that the beads are broken, that she cannot dance tonight, she begins to cry.

I wipe her tears with my hand, say I love her, but she looks confused.

My grandmother doesn't know who I am. She doesn't remember me. But she remembers her beads. How they felt cool on her neck and how they moved against the dark blue of her blouse as she danced.

Fading

It's a frozen February and the curtains are closed against the cold panes of glass. Caitlin shuts her eyes, and she waits, but sleep doesn't come.

There's a wind-up clock on her bedside table. She's never really noticed its ticks and tocks but tonight she hears it and thinks that it's too loud. Daniel is sleeping. She shivers because the sheets have slipped from her shoulder and now she feels cold. But she doesn't move because she doesn't want to wake him. Shadows fall across the floor of the bedroom even though it's dark and she wonders how in the blackness some things can be more dark than others. She watches the shadows move and fade as the hours pass. The tock of the clock fills her ears and this is how she counts the time as it passes. Soon she will have to get up and go to work. She hopes that the library will be quiet when she gets there because she'll be tired and everything will sound louder and closer than it should.

The alarm is set to ring at six-thirty but she picks it up three minutes before it sounds. The metal of the clock feels cold in her hands and she switches it off. Daniel used to laugh at her because the clock is so old. But usually she can't get up without the ringing of its bells. It wakes her with a jump to the heart and then the morning crashes in all at once. Daniel used to laugh at a lot of things, but he doesn't any more. Sometimes she tries to remember when the laughing stopped, but she can't. She puts the clock back on to the cabinet beside the bed: she's glad to get up and shake off the sheets that have tangled around her legs.

The library is busy and loud and she can't concentrate on the tasks she needs to complete. There are children chattering and shouting and running too quickly along the aisles of books. In the afternoon she slams her hand on the counter and shouts, 'Be quiet or get out!' They stop and look at her.

Daniel has two bottles of wine when he comes home. They're red and he has one in each hand. She thinks that this is excessive for a Tuesday but she doesn't say so because she's glad. They're doing this more and more now, the drinking. The wine will make the evening pass faster and maybe the conversation will come more easily. Maybe tonight they will talk like they used to. Maybe tonight it won't be like reciting lines from a play both of them are bored by. At dinner he pours her a drink. He doesn't concentrate and she watches as the wine splashes down the side of her glass. She knows it will stain when it meets the wooden table but she doesn't wipe it up. She looks at his face and asks him about his day.

'How was it?' she asks.

'Fine,' he says, 'how was yours?'

But she doesn't respond because really that's no answer at all. They finish their drinks in silence and he pours them another glass. Later, in the living room she sits on the sofa and he chooses the chair. She watches as he tenses and relaxes his legs and she thinks of the muscles beneath the material of his jeans. He switches on the television and doesn't look at her. She swallows the rest of her wine and then she picks up her book and begins to read.

It's almost midnight when they go upstairs. She washes her face in front of the mirror and thinks that she looks pale. Daniel is already in bed and although they don't touch she can feel the heat from his body. She's wearing a t-shirt and she's cold but she doesn't move towards him. He'll be sleeping soon and she'll be alone. She switches off the lamp. The curtains aren't drawn but tonight she doesn't mind. There's a star in the window, much brighter than the others, and she watches its whiteness in the black sky.

Daniel's breathing is steady and slow. Caitlin listens to his breath as it moves in and out. She counts the seconds of the inhalations and then the exhalations and for a few minutes she tries to mirror them. She notices the movements of his body on the other side of the bed and she thinks he feels far away. She reaches for his hand but she cannot find it.

The next night she knows that she won't sleep as she slides under the sheets of the bed. She closes her eyes. She's never noticed the noise from the road before: the house had always seemed too far back and the walls too thick and solid. She hears engines approach, pass, and then fade. She wonders if she should count them like sheep.

It's four o'clock when she hears the scream. Despite the coolness of the room Caitlin feels a sudden heat. Sweat prickles on her top lip. She wants to wipe it away but doesn't dare move. Then, the noise again, definitely a scream, high pitched and urgent. She pushes back the covers and runs towards the window. The wooden floorboards are cold beneath the soles of her feet.

For a second, through the darkness, she sees nothing. But then at the end of the driveway: a single fox. It paces the pavement, turns sharply, catches sight of something Caitlin can't see. The fox stops and she thinks of hungry dogs and the smell of blood and meat. She watches as it opens its mouth and, again, she hears the scream. A few seconds later she knows that it's a mating call. There are two foxes now and they run and disappear behind hedges that line the park. For a minute she doesn't move. The star she saw from her bed, a few nights before, looks faded and far away now.

Weeks pass and the sky is still frozen and bird-less. She wonders when winter will end and when the colours of the world will come back. There are dark shadows beneath her eyes and today somebody at work asked her if she'd been hit.

'No,' she said. And the noise of the school children nearby made her flinch as she said this. 'I'm just not sleeping, that's all.' And then, 'Is it noisier than usual in here?'

'No,' said Jack and he looked at her in a way she'd never been looked at before.

That night when Daniel is sleeping, she thinks of how they were silent almost all evening. There were a few moments in front of the television when they spoke but when she thinks of them, she realises they were talking to the people on screen. His breathing is loud and slow and deep and then she begins to hear the voices. They're low and whispered and so she can't make out the words.

The voices come from the bedroom next door: they belong to the neighbours. She didn't know Matilda and Luca slept in the adjoining room: she hadn't heard them before. Caitlin lies still and listens. Soon the sound of Luca fades and it's only Matilda's small voice she can hear. A few minutes pass and then there's something rhythmic, a sliding sound, the movement of wood hitting the wall: the sound of a bed rocking back and forth. Caitlin's face feels hot. Her palms sweat.

Her day at work passes slowly but finally it's late and she can leave. The library is dusky: the colours dulled by the darkening sky. It's empty aside from one man. He often comes here but they've never spoken. She wonders if this evening she will have to tell him to leave, wonders if this evening he will finally look at her.

'Fuck,' she hears his voice across the library and then scrabbling as he picks up his things and runs towards the door. He passes the counter. Caitlin notices the handles of his heavy shopping bags and how they dig into his palms. She knows what's inside. She'd stood behind him earlier and had smelled oranges and lemons she couldn't see. She'd been so close that she could hear his breath but she knew he hadn't noticed her. She watches as he runs down the street, wonders what he is late for, wonders who he is late for.

Later, at home, it's the early hours when she begins to hear them. Through the wall she hears the movement of the bed again: springs being pressed and squeezed and the sound of sheets rising and falling. She can feel her heart beating faster. She imagines that they're kissing now. That Luca's kissing Matilda's hot mouth and her face and breathing into her ears. She imagines that he's kissing Matilda's neck and then lower and lower still. She imagines that Matilda's skin is soft and pale and that the stubble on Luca's face feels rough, but good as he moves his lips along her stomach and her sides and her back. And then there's the rhythmic sliding sound again and the bounce of the bedhead on the wall that separates them.

Caitlin climbs from her bed. She puts her head against the wall to listen more closely. She feels the raised flock of the paper beneath her palm and steadies her balance with her foot. The rhythm is faster now and then faster again and she presses her ear closer until she can feel the bricks beneath the paper. For a few minutes she doesn't move.

Then the sound stops and there's stillness. She wonders if there was the feeling of being watched. She wonders if they imagined someone standing at the side of their bed and if they did, whether they liked it. There's whispering again and the sound of sheets being pushed back. She thinks of Matilda's naked breasts: how they would look pale and blue in the morning light, and she imagines Luca naked too.

Daniel turns over. She watches his movement and the way his chest grows as he breathes. Maybe he's awake? Her legs feel weak, watery. She wants him to pick her up. She wants him to take her back to bed, to hold her, to notice that she is there. But now he's still again and his breathing sounds like sleep.

The voices next door rise for a second and it seems as though they're speaking to her. Caitlin moves her head and feels the coldness of the wall. Then there is silence again and she is alone.

Leaving

Joe was home at seven, which meant he'd stayed after work for a coffee or a beer. Sarah guessed it was a beer but he never said. There'd been a vagueness to him for months now, parts of him missing and lost to her, and she was getting used to the guessing. She'd tried to remember when it first started but it happened slowly, creeping in silently for weeks. And now this evening it was here and it was definite. She could see that he was leaving. It was in the lines around his mouth.

He hadn't said anything as he walked through the front door, but lit a cigarette and sat at the kitchen table. He played with his silver cigarette box.

'How was your day?' she asked.

'Fine,' he said, 'I'm surprised you're home. Don't you normally see your sister on a Thursday?' He looked dark under the eyes and his mouth was set, hard. There was a chicken cooking in the oven and she turned away to check the browning bird behind the glass door. He'd left the room when she turned back to face him, silently without even the noise of his boots on the floor.

She heard the shower being switched on and noticed how the splashes changed their pace as he climbed in and under the hot spikes of running water. His mobile phone was on the table. She picked it up and carefully entered the pin number she saw him tap in a week ago.

Sarah searched through the phone menu and selected messages. She scanned the lines of text and found a name that she recognised: Lisa. Lisa who she'd gone to school with, Lisa who she'd known for most of her life. She scanned again and found lines of pleas and encouragement, of secrets and longing, and of words meant to lead him away.

Sarah walked to the bathroom. The shower was hot, the window closed and steam filled the tiny space. She held the mobile phone face up in her palm and he saw its glowing screen. There was a second where his face moved in a way she recognised, but then there was nothing: blankness. He turned away and stood with his back to her.

'I want to know when it started,' she said quietly. There was silence as her words disappeared in to the white, wet air. She hoped they would touch him, like something sharp being dragged across his skin, to spur him to apologies or tears.

'Seven and a half months ago,' said Joe. And then he told her all the details she asked to hear. He told her about the places they met and how he loved her dark hair and red shoes. He told her how, over coffee, he held Lisa's hand and kissed her neck. He told Sarah slowly, like he was at work, simplifying a complicated task for a colleague. It was as if they were strangers and she hated him.

There was a feeling she'd never had before: an urge to hurt him and it tightened across her chest. She stepped forward and pushed him. The floor of the shower was slippery with soap and Joe stumbled but managed to stay on his feet. He banged his head on the tiles and a wet stain of red appeared at his temple. The blood streamed and splashed into the water, pooled pink around his feet. For a second he was blind. Sarah watched his crouched body beneath the running water. Then she reached for the temperature gauge of the shower. She pushed it around to the red section of the thermostat and held it there. It was the first time she'd heard a man scream.

'You fucking bitch,' he shouted. He pushed her hard against the wall, paused for a second, had a look in his eyes she'd never seen before. She held her breath, waited and then he let her go.

He got dressed even though he was still wet and started to pack a bag. Sarah sat on a stool in front of her dressing table and looked at him through the mirror. In spite of Lisa, she didn't want him to leave. She didn't want to start again with a stranger.

'Please stay,' she said.

'It's too fucking late,' he said. 'Let's not make this more difficult than it needs to be.' He'd looked at her face then as if it was all her fault. And so for a few seconds she'd closed her eyes. Maybe she'd imagined it. Maybe this wasn't real after all. Except when she opened them again she saw he'd packed socks, shirts, jeans, his work uniform.

'Don't forget your toothbrush from the bathroom,' she said.

'Keep it,' he said, 'I'll ring you to arrange coming for the rest of my things.'

The house felt still and cool after he left and she noticed the sound of her bare feet on the carpet.

Later, Sarah phoned Joe's mother. She was sure he would stay there until they worked this out. It was a long drive, especially in the dark and maybe he was upset. She should check on him: she should make sure he was okay.

The phone rang four times.

'Hello.'

'Hello, it's Sarah,' she said. 'I've called to speak to Joe.' There was a pause.

'Joe isn't here,' said Joe's mum and then, 'is everything okay?

'No,' said Sarah, 'Joe's been sleeping with Lisa. You know, my friend Lisa. We had a fight. I pushed him and he hit his head in the shower. I should never have let him drive in that state but I just wasn't thinking.'

'Oh, God,' Joe's mum said, 'he isn't here.'

'Do you think he's at Lisa's?' asked Sarah, though it wasn't really a question now, because of course that's where he would be. Lisa would be soothing his aching head and kissing his neck and saying, look this just proves it: you really did make the right choice didn't you. Still I'd never have expected *that* from Sarah.

'I don't know,' said Joe's mother, 'but I'm sorry and I'm sure it'll all work out.' She clicked the receiver on to its cradle then, before Sarah could speak and there was silence on the line.

Sarah waits for Joe. She's in a supermarket car park: a halfway point, chosen by him. People push past the car, zigzagging across the painted tarmac with trolleys full of shopping. Her car is full of his things. His clothes are folded neatly into bags, his favourite mugs and ornaments are placed safely in to boxes lined up on the seats of her car. A bag of his clothes sits beside her. Even though she's washed them they smell of him and the scent of his scarf, pulled from the bag and wrapped around her hand, almost drives her mad. She wishes she was angry, but everything aches.

Five minutes late, Joe pulls into the car park. She's parked where he asked, next to a flower bed full of snow drops and old coke cans. She waits for Joe to get out of his car. He lightly taps the driver side window to get her attention, as if she were here for any other reason than for him. It's cold when she gets out of the car and she can smell bread from the in-store bakery. She can't think of anything to say, so in silence hands over his boxes and bags. When they've finished he says thank you like a stranger and looks at her mouth. Her bottom lip shakes as he watches.

A mutual friend had already told her and Sarah asks Joe if it's true. He nods slowly and says yes – we're getting married. Sarah doesn't think he deserves a happy ever after and her throat burns.

'I'm so happy,' he says and then tells her that she is the type of woman who watches as the world passes her by. He climbs into his car and the keys in her hand dig into her palm.

It's two months later now and Sarah is at home. One of the kitchen taps is leaking and she can hear the water fall in heavy drops to the silver sink. She's writing a birthday card. It's for a man she works with. She thinks of earlier that day and how taking a piece of paper from her, he touched her hand. She'd felt the warmth of his skin for a second and she thinks about the lines of his palms. It's his birthday next week and she has already wrapped his present. As a thank you, he will give her a hug. He will squeeze her tightly around the shoulders and pull her chest towards him. She will breathe in his aftershave and the smell of his skin. Then his wedding ring will dig in to her shoulder blade and a few seconds later he will let her go.

The Hottest Day

The air smelt of sweet meat and smouldering coals. It was early evening and new guests arrived for food and dancing. A *Congratulations Lucy and Dave* banner hung across the heavy doors of the country house and balloons bounced on the grass in the breeze. A man in a white hat and apron put orange chicken wings on to a barbeque and the sauce started flickers of fresh flame.

George picked up another drink from the free bar. He didn't know most of the people, all dressed in their best outfits. The old friends and distant family who smiled at the happy couple were mostly strangers. The crowd laughed and George listened as they reminisced about old times and new futures. George slipped to the edge of the room. For a whole year he'd hoped she'd change her mind and choose him.

His suit felt itchy in this heat. It was the hottest day of the year and nobody had predicted it. The band had moved outside to the grass at the last minute according to his brother Dave, who had undone his waistcoat and cravat. Dave drank something fizzy and pink from a long glass with ice. George's collar felt tight around his neck. He undid some buttons and looked at his brother, who, aside from the different clothes, was a mirror. A late arrival with a silver package in his arms wandered along the driveway towards the crowd and Dave disappeared with him to find his wife.

People had been drinking all afternoon. The crowd was noisier than before. A small boy kicked and pushed another, snatching his blue box of sweets. There was a box at every setting earlier, laid on serviettes between silver knives and sparkling glass. The smaller boy screamed. A woman pushed through the crowd and pulled the silent boy to the shade of a tree. The bow on the box was undone and had fallen to the floor. She smacked his leg.

'Calm down,' she shouted. And then he cried.

There was a couple kissing close to the marquee. The woman wore a dress with no straps and had taken off her shoes. Her shoulders were damp with sweat and looked like wax in the sun. George thought of shop window mannequins. For a second she pulled away and looked at the man's teeth. He must have bitten her lip because she put her hand on her mouth and checked her fingers for blood. Nothing: and so she kissed him again.

George went inside for another drink. A group of his brother's friends were at the bar buying shots. They got him one too and then disappeared outside to smoke cigars in the sunshine.

George leant against the bar. His palms were sweaty and he rubbed his hands on his trousers. When he'd looked up, Lucy's mum was in front of him. She'd taken off her hat: she looked younger, looked good. Lucy was like her. She got another drink and they both sat down. She was drunk and her words were slow and slurred. She asked George if he was enjoying himself and he said not really because he didn't know that many people and he hadn't spoken to Lucy today. Well, just once and she'd only smiled at him.

'She's always been a spoilt bitch. I blame her father. She lived with him after we split up.'

George didn't think she was spoilt but he thought about taking her mother to his hotel room. She put her hand on his thigh and he decided he wanted her. He leant forward and told her his room number. He remembered from the speeches that her name was Katy. Her skin smelt different to Lucy's but Lucy was there: in the curve of Katy's shoulders and the red of her mouth. It was just enough. Maybe it would be like when Lucy took him home.

It happened two weeks after his brother introduced them. They'd both finished work late: it was early evening. He met her at the bar buying a bottle of wine to take away. He said hello and she said it had been a rough day. It would be nice to talk and she couldn't get hold of his brother on the phone. She'd said that work had been stressful although he doesn't remember why now and he'd offered her a cigarette. She'd said yes and they'd gone outside.

For a few minutes they'd smoked quietly together and he'd watched how her shoulders moved when she exhaled. They'd talked about work and about the weather and they'd laughed. Then suddenly it was much later and the music was louder. She'd stood closer to him and he'd talked into her ear. He remembers that it was dark and that there were stars and she touched his cheek. Her finger was cold and so he held her hand. Then they went back to her house and she took him to bed.

It was light when she asked him to leave, although George could still see the crescent of the moon through her bedroom window. She put on her pyjamas and waited for him in the hallway. She held him as he stood on the doorstep.

'I'm so sorry, George,' she said, 'it was a mistake. You do understand that don't you?'

But it wasn't really a question. 'I'll see you out,' said Lucy. She stood in the doorway and watched him walk down the path.

It was a long walk home and the morning was cold. He could hear birds, a milk float in the next street, dogs whining behind locked gates.

It was six months later when Dave told George that him and Lucy were getting married. George was silent. Then he smiled and said, 'Congratulations Dave.' He wanted to say how he'd been in love with Lucy since that time he smoked with her. He wanted to tell him how he whispered into her ear and held her cold hand until it was warm like his. But he didn't because there was a look on his brother's face he hadn't seen before.

George was back outside now – he'd left Katy in his hotel room. It was still early but people were already dancing in the marquee. He stood on the grass and watched from the door. The sun was hot and the music, too loud for this time of day, beat in his chest. He wiped the sweat from his forehead, loosened the collar from his neck. The dancing crowd in the tent had blurred beneath the rainbow of disco lights and then there was Lucy, who'd walked over to his brother in her white dress and bare feet and held his hand.

You could hear the crunch of gravel as he walked along the driveway. Birds watched from trees that pierced the blue sky. He took a breath as he stopped at the heavy gate, turned right into the road and quietly disappeared from view.

Laughter

We met at the town hall. Jim had a banner too and chanted slogans about freedom and fairness. I thought he was like me.

Often I think of him, the lines of his teeth when he smiled, the sound of his laugh and how, suddenly, he went away.

I stood at the gate and watched him go. There was a frost and my toes ached in my thin socks. He turned back to wave and I smiled, and my grin was almost as big as his. A second later the curve of the road hid him from view and I never saw him again.

We'd been dating for a year. I remember his voice and the way he touched me, and I cannot believe he lied for so long and with such an honest face.

Jim, the undercover policeman with a smile that wasn't even his.

Now I'm alone and I know what my neighbours' laughter sounds like through the walls. And I cry and I say Jim's name, as if that will make a difference.

Umbrella

Peter saw the whole thing as it happened. He saw the man come out of the coffee shop on the corner in his smart work clothes and then the kid as he ran down the street. He heard the noise as the kid's fist broke the bones of the man's nose and he saw the blood come suddenly like somebody had turned on a tap. Peter could tell by the direction of the man's eyes that he was looking at stars straight away. For a few seconds the man managed to stay on his feet and Peter was surprised. Then the kid lurched forward and Peter saw the silver flash of a blade disappear beneath the man's ribs.

It took a second for the crimson stain to spread across the man's shirt and then Peter watched as he folded and fell to the floor. The kid had the man's laptop bag in his hand now and, as he ran past, Peter saw he was still holding the knife.

A crowd started to gather around the man on the floor. It was raining and no one had thought to stop him from getting wet. Peter went over and held out his umbrella.

He usually felt lucky to work this street, to have this particular spot. It was closed to cars and he could stand right in the middle. It was narrow enough to stride the whole width in a few seconds. People knew his face now. They liked how he was polite even when his feet were frozen and his hands ached from cold. Most weeks he sold enough magazines to pay his room rent and some weeks enough to buy tobacco and a tin of beer or two.

The man's blood ran across the pavement and Peter could smell it. There was a metallic taste in his mouth and he swallowed to make it go. A woman from the coffee shop had come outside. She knelt on the wet concrete, held the man's hand. She asked him his name and he said it was Mathew.

'Everything will be okay, Mathew,' she said, 'we've called an ambulance and they'll be here soon.' The rain rolled down Peter's jacket. A few minutes passed and his arm ached from holding the umbrella so still in the air. Mathew started to speak then.

'Look,' said Mathew, 'the sky has turned orange. I've never seen it that colour before, what does it mean?' Nobody told him it was the fabric of an umbrella. Nobody knew if he was dying or not except it looked like he was and if a man was going to die on a pavement in a dirty street, and thought that the sky had turned orange, maybe they should just let him think that.

Peter stopped listening. He hadn't heard a man talk that way for a long time and even though it was years ago now he couldn't help but think of those moments with other men. Not moments exactly, but times maybe, when there had been sand and guns and wars he didn't understand. He'd signed up with lads from school and he doubted any of them were still alive now, even the ones who got home.

One he'd seen ripped apart by a roadside bomb in the early hours of a Sunday morning. One had been shot in the back somewhere in a desert he'd forgotten the name of. The other three had made it home but he'd watched them on tour as they'd all become less and less of themselves until finally, when they were released from duty, there was really nothing of them left. He sometimes wondered what those wars meant now. Probably nothing at all.

Peter watched the blur of passing people and tried to stop thinking of the blood and the rain that pooled around his feet and soaked into his boots. The rain ran down his face and his hat was wet. He could feel the heaviness in the wool and his head itched. He pulled his nails quickly across his forehead and a sharp edge snagged his skin. He took the hat from his head and pushed it into his pocket. It'd been months since he'd got this wet: not since the woman had handed him her umbrella. He wondered where she was now and if she ever thought of him when it rained.

That day the rain had been heavy and cold. By lunchtime Peter couldn't feel his toes anymore. He didn't have a watch but could count the time with the passing of the crowd: early morning commuters and coffee drinkers, people leaving offices for cigarettes and sandwiches at lunch and then tired, faded faces going home at just after five. That day was Sunday, though and Sundays were different. Time was slow. Everyone drifted through the city with no place to be and no deadline to be there.

The streets were less crowded and his feet ached following the few people he saw from one side of the road to the other. He just needed to get rid of a few more copies and then he could go home. He stamped his feet. And then there was a woman walking towards him. She looked at him and said, 'Do you want this?' tilting her umbrella towards him. Peter said, 'Yeah, if you're giving it away,' and he searched her face, looked away. Sometimes people joked about giving him their things. Sometimes it was a dare in front of their friends or sometimes it was for nobody else's benefit but their own.

He didn't move, waited, avoided her eyes. Silently she handed it over, put up the hood of her coat and then turned and walked in the direction she'd come from.

When he wrapped his fingers around the handle, it felt warm in his hands and he hadn't expected he would notice anything like that. Except it was the closest he'd come to being touched in a long time and he couldn't stop thinking about it for days.

Fire

She is hot and restless and through her dreams she begins to hear a noise. It's quiet at first but soon it's louder and louder again and then she's awake, pulled from her dreaming.

Astrid opens her eyes: the fire alarm rings high above the bed. The hotel room is dark. She reaches for the watch she placed on the bedside table a few hours before. Its face says two a.m. Her eyes begin to adjust to the blackness around her and the contents of the room appear: a desk with a lamp standing on it, a high-sided chair in the corner, and long curtains, not fully drawn, frame a window. Robin feels warm beside her. She reaches for him and touches his shoulder. He's lying on his side facing her and she can feel his breath on her neck. There's the smell of rum from the night before and she thinks of the good time they had celebrating her new job. Last night she'd decided it was a fun city and she was excited to move somewhere new.

'Robin, are you awake?' she asks.

'How could I not be with that noise?' he says.

'Do you think we should get up?'

'It's probably a false alarm,' he says, 'just wait for a few minutes. I'm sure we'll be able to go back to sleep.' She looks through the darkness and the whites of his eyes disappear as he closes his lids.

'We should check,' she says. 'I'll go and have a look in the corridor.'

'I have a headache,' he says. 'This noise is really not helping.' Astrid picks up her jacket and pushes her arms into the sleeves. The material is cold. This is always the worst thing about getting up in the morning.

The corridor is dark but she can see outlines of other people standing in the doorways of their rooms.

'The electricity has gone off,' says a voice to her left. 'I wonder if that's why the alarm has sounded?'

'So you think it's a false alarm?' she asks.

'Maybe,' he says, 'I hope so, but who knows?' For a few seconds nobody speaks and the corridor is still. Astrid's ribs feel tight and they make her breath shallow. She breathes quickly now.

Then, through the darkness, there's another voice. Astrid can see a woman's dark shadow move down the centre of the corridor.

'There's smoke in the main stairwell,' says the woman, 'and it's rising. We need to get out.'

Astrid steps back inside the bedroom. She notices how the carpet changes beneath her feet and the thickness of the pile slows her as she walks to the side of the bed. They're on the seventh floor and she wonders how many stairs there are to walk or run down before they will reach the ground outside.

'Robin, it's not a false alarm,' she says, 'there's a fire.' She watches the darkness move as he sits up and she begins to get dressed. She pulls on her trousers, pushes her bare feet into Converse. The canvas catches and rubs on her heels. She fumbles with the laces.

'Robin,' her voice is higher now, 'I can smell the smoke, please move.'

'Okay, I'm getting up,' he says. 'You know what I'm like in the morning.' He laughs and Astrid begins to cough.

'You're still drunk, Robin, and it's not funny. I can't breathe.' The smoke surrounds them now – it only took a few minutes to reach their room. Robin fumbles with his jeans and falls. 'Are you okay?' Astrid is shouting now.

'Go, go! I'll be right behind you,' Robin says. He stands again and searches for Astrid through the black. He finds her shoulder and pushes her through the doorway. The corridor is crowded: bedroom doors are open and people move quickly along the hallway. People push and surge as she is thrown in to the crowd.

They follow the EXIT signs through the darkness. Astrid hears a child crying and someone begins to shout, *For God's sake, hurry up*. Smoke swirls in the green glow of the EXIT signs. It's thick and smells of burning plastic and rubber. Someone is sick behind her. She hears the retching and the wetness as it hits the floor and then there's a burning in her throat. She puts her hand over her mouth and notices that her lips are dry and tight. Then, ahead is the door to the fire escape. Someone pushes it open and through the smoke there's the smell of the night outside. The crowd push quicker towards the door.

The staircase is a zigzag at the side of the building. She can hear the noise of shoes on metal now and the sound of bare feet as they slap the cool steel. The sky is close and black and the city seems a long way down. The fallen stars of shops and streetlights shine yellow and blue below her.

The staircase shakes beneath the weight of the crowd. Astrid looks up at the people above her but they move too quickly and she can't make out if Robin is there. The fire assembly point is across the street: staff in uniform stand with their arms in the air. They are shouting and telling the crowd to assemble beneath a streetlight that flickers pink because it's broken.

She's almost at the bottom of the stairs now. She notices again that the canvas of her Converse shoes rubs the heels of her bare feet. She looks down at them. They're zebra print with silver stripes. She loved them as soon as she saw them. They were a birthday present from Robin last year and she thinks that the blisters are worth it.

Astrid's skin is sticky and hot: it's the middle of the city and the concrete and steel have held on to the heat from the hot days before. The pavement is cracked beneath her feet and blue forget-me-nots grow through the gaps. Astrid looks at their wilted, dry leaves. She thinks of greenness and space and wonders if she'll ever have the chance to leave crowded cities behind. She checks the stairs and the crowd of faces that streams down them. No Robin yet.

A woman next to her takes a packet of cigarettes from her dressing gown pocket. When the cigarette is in her mouth she clicks an orange lighter. The flame is set too high and it almost catches her nose. The smoke of the cigarette coils across the woman's face and rushes towards the sky. Astrid wonders how the woman can smoke so soon after leaving the burning building.

There are children in the crowd and some of them are crying.

'Look,' says a boy with bare feet, 'look at the birds. Are they flying away from the fire?'

Astrid looks at the sky and sees the black shadows of bats there. She counts three. They swoop and fall towards the crowd gathered on the street. Usually this space would be theirs at this time of night and she wonders if they are angry at the crowd for being there. More of them come, maybe there are six now, though they're difficult to count and, every now and then she hears their high-pitched squeaks. Others begin to notice and soon somebody from across the crowd screams.

The fire escape is emptier now. Astrid can see through the gaps between the black spiral of the steps. There's graffiti that she didn't notice on the way down. There are thick letters in pink and blue and words in yellow and red that she can't quite read. The layers of paint look pretty against the dirty grey of the concrete wall.

She should be able to see Robin. She scans the faces around her, checks the heads and the shoulders, the jackets and pyjamas. She doesn't see him. The last of the staff in their red shirts and name badges step onto the pavement. She sees that the stairs are empty now: she sees that nobody else is coming.

Anywhere Else But There

There was a song Ben heard once sung by a beautiful black woman whose name he couldn't remember. She sang about strange fruit hanging from the branches of trees. He'd had that song in his head for weeks now.

Maybe the postman was new, maybe he wasn't quite awake yet, but as Ben left for work there was a letter on the mat that didn't belong to him. He picked up the envelope and closed the front door. He'd give it to Leon before he left for work.

That was months ago now and the last time Ben saw Leon alive. The morning had been dark. Car lights flashed orange and red through glassy baubles of rain. Leon's house was across the road - the number eighty-two displayed by the door on a wooden plaque. He lived there with his girlfriend Ruby who looked tired and who sometimes smiled at Ben but never spoke. Not many of the neighbours did: they were always busy, rushing to be somewhere else, hoping to get there sooner than the traffic would probably allow.

As he walked along Leon's garden path he could see through the front room window. Leon was on the phone and Ben gestured to the letter in his hand. Leon gave him a thumbs up and mouthed thank you as he pointed to the letter box. As Ben pushed it through the door he noticed that the letter was stamped with a red *Final Notice*. The house was tidy and ordinary and Leon looked like he always did when they passed on the street.

Ben stood and looked from the window of his upstairs bedroom. It was spring and the sun was bright and hot through the glass. After a minute it had begun to burn his face. A tree in the garden had white bulbs on its branches and the petals pointed upwards like church candles. He loved magnolia: the trees were beautiful until there was rain. It made him sad to see the flowers collapse beneath the weight of the water and fall from the branches like giant confetti. The grass was dark and the trees were full of thick, heavy leaves. It was a good view from here: Ben could see the neighbours' gardens and into the fields behind. The sky was wide and open and sometimes, on a quiet, still day, it didn't feel like a city at all.

Leon had been missing for ten days: one evening he just hadn't come home. He was usually back by six and Ruby had called the police when, at midnight, there was still no sign of him. She'd called his mobile over and over again. At first there had been ringing but later the automated voice of his answerphone clicked straight in: maybe the battery was flat, maybe he was somewhere where the signal was bad.

Ben remembered the song. He hadn't heard it for years and he thought of fruit trees and the one that was full of apples in Mr Patel's garden three doors down. The fruit was big enough to see from his window and a crisp, bright green. The window was open and he could smell grass that had just been cut. Slowly Ben's eyes settled on a shape close to the apple tree. It was a shadow at first. But then he saw the faint form of a body; limp legs, heavy shoulders. He looked harder and found a face, feet that weren't touching the ground.

For a long time Ben didn't move.

When a bird hovered for a second close to the hanging man, he ran downstairs, out of the front door and down the street to number sixty-two. The pavement rushed beneath his feet in flashes of white and navy paving stones and glitter that caught the sun.

Number sixty-two had a light blue door and he hammered on the wood. The skin on his knuckles split and blood smudged on the paintwork. There was no answer.

The back gate was rotten and felt soft as Ben jumped over it. He knew it was too late for the man hanging from the tree but he kept running, didn't slow down.

A tight band of blue rope dug deep across Leon's neck: his face a bruised purple of trapped blood. His shirtsleeve was pulled up and Ben could see his watch. Its white dial was bright in the light of the sun and it still ticked the time.

Ben pulled his phone from his pocket and dialled 999. When the operator asked who he wanted, he hesitated. He knew it was too late and that there was nothing an ambulance could do. But still, it didn't feel right to be the first person to decide.

He told the woman on the phone that Leon was hanging from the branch of a fruit tree. His voice shook and faded to a whisper. Ben sat down. The operator said that the police would be with him in a few minutes and that he should try to remain calm. There was nothing he could do now except sit tight and keep talking to her until they arrived. The woman on the phone had an accent and he wondered where it was from.

The world felt still and he looked at Leon's shoes. They hung above the ground, only their shadow touching the grass.

When the police car arrived, people appeared in doorways and watched as Leon, cut from the branches and zipped in a clean, neat bag, was put into the back of a van. Ben could hear the noise of birds now and the voices of the neighbours.

Less than two weeks later Ruby left the house across the road. She put Leon's clothes and shoes into bags and then she left them on the street for anyone who wanted them. Ben watched as she dragged the bags from her front door, across the driveway and onto the pavement of the street. She looked at the floor and didn't raise her eyes across the narrow road to the houses in front of her.

Mr Patel had been away seeing family and didn't come back until Ruby had moved out. The police said there was no suggestion he was involved. Maybe Leon just liked the view from Mr Patel's back garden better: the view out across the fields where, on a good day, you could look up into the wide, open sky and pretend you were anywhere else but there.

Shoes

The car park is busy. It's level seven before Abi finds a space. It doesn't really matter today, she isn't in a hurry.

The shoes are perched on a ledge: she sees them from her car window. She parks, gets out, and goes back to look at them.

She thinks they look neat, placed there side by side. They're Converse: black with silver stars. The sun catches them, the silver sparkles.

She picks one up: size four, her size. She wonders why they're here on the ledge, wonders if she should take them, wonders if anyone is coming back. The noise of the city below rises. There's graffiti on the walls.

Abi steps towards the ledge and picks up the other shoe. They feel light in her hands, small. She looks down and then she sees her: a woman twisted and still and with no shoes on her pale, bare feet.

She Picks Up the Cat

She picks up the cat, climbs the stairs and closes the bathroom door softly behind her. She puts him down and slides the lock into place. He pads about on the lino and looks at her. She knows he doesn't like the coolness beneath his paws but, for now, he will have to be patient. She runs the hot tap and steam begins to cloud the mirror above the sink.

The website says: pack an emergency bag for yourself and hide it somewhere safe. She wiggles the bath panel loose, slides it out enough to fit her arm inside the gap, searches for the material of the bag. There: it's in her hand and she pulls it out.

Be prepared to leave the house in an emergency. She isn't sure exactly what this means, though she has money on her at all times, like it says. Change for the phone, for bus fare. It's inside her bra.

She can hear the banging downstairs, the crockery smashing. She imagines the shards of blue plates joining the broken glass dish, the teapot, the coffee cups.

If you suspect that your partner is about to attack you, go to a lower risk area of the house, go to somewhere you can find a way out. Avoid the kitchen or garage where there will be knives and other weapons.

She thinks of the knife block, how he knocked it over, chose the one with the serrated blade, brushed her face with its point. How close: how easy it would've been for him to press harder, to pull it slowly across her skin. She avoided his eyes, watched as he turned and threw the knife across the kitchen, watched as its handle hit the cat and felt lucky it wasn't the blade.

The bath is half full now. She pushes the bathroom window wide, looks down to the flat roof below and the back gate that is slightly ajar.

Avoid rooms where you might be trapped, such as the bathroom, or where you might be shut into a cupboard or other small spaces. She quietly clicks the bath panel back into place, thinks of the darkness behind, the space like a coffin.

The bag is on her back now, the cat in her arms. She hears his footsteps on the stairs, looks at the door and hopes that the lock will hold.

Acknowledgements

Some of these stories were published elsewhere. A version of 'Bones' was featured in the anthology *High Spirits: A Round of Drinking Stories* published by Valley Press; a version of 'The Best Way to Kill A Butterfly' was featured in *Unthology 10: Fight or Flight*, published by Unthank Books; a version of 'The Soft Broken parts' under the title 'Man Under' was published in Brilliant Flash Fiction; a version of 'Ragdoll' was published by Fictive Dream; a version of 'Anywhere Else But There' under the title 'Ten Days Missing' was published by Idle Ink; a version of 'The Call of the Circus' was published by X-R-A-Y Literary Magazine; 'The Ypres Cross' was published on the Creative Writing at Leicester blog; 'She Picks Up the Cat,' was published by Fairlight Books; a version of 'Gabriel' was published by Losslit Magazine; versions of 'The Moon Was Low and Close' and 'When the Sun Sets' were published by The Letterpress Project; a version of 'Swings' was published on FlashFlood; a version of 'Strawberry Fields' under the name 'Anderson's Strawberry Farm,' and 'Caterpillars,' 'Robin,' 'Shoes' and 'Wasp,' were all published in various editions of *The New Luciad*.

About the Author

Hannah Stevens is a writer from Leicester, England. She has published fiction and creative nonfiction in literary journals and anthologies internationally. A PhD in creative writing from the University of Leicester, she has taught writing at various universities across the world. *In their Absence* is her debut book.

Milton Keynes UK
Ingram Content Group UK Ltd.
UKHW040213160324
439374UK00004B/217